THE CABIN
AT
MEDICINE SPRINGS

THE CABIN
AT
MEDICINE
SPRINGS

LULITA CRAWFORD PRITCHETT

Illustrated by
Anthony D'Adamo

FRANKLIN WATTS, INCORPORATED, NEW YORK

First Printing
Library of Congress Catalog Card Number: 58-9973
Copyright © 1958 by Lulita Crawford Pritchett
All Rights Reserved
Manufactured in the United States of America by
Montauk Book Manufacturing Company, Inc.

ILLUSTRATIONS

THE CABIN
AT
MEDICINE SPRINGS

CHAPTER I

Something had scared the milk cows that June evening in 1879. Lulie, twelve, and Logan, nine, had almost run their legs off trying to drive them into the corral on the bank of Bear River; and Spy, the black-and-white shepherd dog, had chased bawling runaways till the sweat dripped off her tongue.

Usually the cows plodded in of their own accord, with Spot, the bell cow, leading the way down the trail they had made from Lookout Hill, across a brushy bench, and through the draw to the log enclosure. Tonight they acted as though they had no idea where the corral was.

Lulie tossed the hair out of her face. One long, dark braid had come undone, but she could not stop to braid it. "Go home, Brin—Star!" she gasped. "What's got into you?"

"Maybe that wolf came back," panted Logan.

A few nights ago the children had found the cows bunched in a circle, their flashing horns defying a lean, gray marauder that was trying to dart at a newborn calf in the middle of the circle. Lulie and Logan had thrown sticks at the wolf, and Spy had made a brave rush, and it had loped up the gulch.

Now, peering intently through the sunset glow, Lulie

could see only familiar sagebrush and, higher up on the ridge, the copper of new oak leaves and the mist of choke-cherry bloom. From the little hill above the cabin where she stood, she could look over the tops of the long-leaved cottonwoods lining Soda Creek to the meadows and willow patches of the broad valley beyond. Her alert eyes caught no movement except the fluttering of small birds hunting roosting places in the bushes and the glimmer of swal-lows' wings against the dark background of Storm Moun-tain.

In the other direction she could see pink clouds reflected in the pond formed by several of the mineral springs. The pond was the busiest spot in the valley these days. Ducks, muskrats, and beaver made trails across it. Snipe and rails skirted the shallows. Even now, at dusk, a clamor arose from the tangled reeds surrounding it, topped by the chor-tling of red-winged blackbirds. Between the pond and the cabin, and along the base of the hill, there lay a rumpled sea of dark-green rushes, among which the springs glinted. Each spring had built a mound for itself, presided over by dozens of frogs that added their voices to the evening chorus. Lulie could see or hear nothing unusual.

Just before Pa had left for Outside, he and Uncle Henry had driven the stock home from winter range in Burns's Hole. Though the cows had all been wild at first, and were still a little wild, they had never acted like this.

Ponto, Spy's half-grown yellow puppy, who seemed to have a notion that all this cow-chasing was a game, grabbed his mother with playful jaws. She nipped him sharply and stood aquiver.

"What is it, Spy?" whispered Lulie.

Through the winter months the mountains had towered like protectors over the Crawfords' log-cabin home, but with the spring "breakup" they were no longer great walls rimming a world which was for the most part silent and sleeping. Travelers were again abroad. Bears came nightly to the mineral marshes to hunt frogs, as their oozy tracks in the mud proclaimed. Deer had trailed up from winter range in the lower country, and elk were in all the groves, eating the juicy aspen twigs. The skyways had been filled with sandhill cranes and geese and ducks returning.

It was good to see blue wood smoke coming out of the stovepipe of the cabin, where Ma was cooking supper. There was no other smoke in the valley. Though Uncle Henry Crawford had built a cabin on the other side of the creek, he and his wife and baby had gone to spend the summer at Hahn's Peak, twenty-five miles north, to placer for gold.

It was good to see the flag on the peeled pine pole halfway between the cabin and the Iron Spring, its thirteen stripes and thirty-eight stars catching the last warm light from the west. The flag was a fine large one that friends in Missouri had sent Pa.

The corral seemed an endless distance away. If Pa had been home, he would have come to help, but he had gone Outside nearly a month ago to haul in a load of provisions and had not yet returned. Ordinarily Dave, a husky Negro lad from Missouri who was working for Pa, would have been here, but he was carrying mail from Rock Creek till the contractor at Hot Sulphur Springs in Middle Park could hire another carrier. Tenderfeet did not last long in this frontier land, its creeks and rivers booming with the run-off from snow on the range.

The cows kinked their tails and started for Denver, heavy bags swinging.

"Head 'em off, John!" shrilled Lulie.

Six-year-old John, his red hair a spot of flame above his round freckled face, shooed the miscreants valiantly while Ma, running from the cabin, waved her apron. Finally the herd bulged into the corral.

Logan slid the poles across the gate. "There," he panted, "reckon that'll hold you!"

He and Lulie grabbed their buckets and stools and set to milking as fast as they could, and Ma, a rosy little woman with bright dark eyes, put supper on the back of the stove and came to help.

Fleet and Fanny, the twin fawns, squeezed under the fence and ran to Brin, who had been their foster mother ever since Logan had found them in the willows. Usually Brin did not mind giving them their dinner. Tonight she kicked at them. She kicked at her own calf.

"Shame on you, Brin!" scolded Ma. "What is the matter with these cows!"

Lulie pressed her head against a warm red flank. "So-o-o, Spot," she murmured. Above the scuff of hoofs and rattle of pails she was aware of whisperings in the cottonwoods, and the roar of creek and river. She felt a need to hurry.

By the time the milking was finished and the milk strained through snowy cloths and put away in pans in the milkhouse, it was dark except for a golden streak over Elk Mountain. The noises in the marsh had subsided. Only a lonesome killdeer cried.

Tobe and Tabby, the big gray cats, crouched by their pan, up to their whiskers in white foam. Ponto had already finished his milk. Spy would not drink. She stood in the cabin doorway, shivering.

"What's the matter, Spy?" Lulie asked.

CHAPTER II

Lulie was glad to get inside the sturdy log walls of the kitchen, where candlelight pushed back the shadows and where she could hear the throaty song of the teakettle on the stove.

"Logan," said Ma, "did you shut up the chickens?"

Ma had only six hens left. Skunks, mink, and foxes had made off with the rest.

"Yes'm. All but Tommy."

Tommy was a spoiled red-gold bantam with green neck feathers; he had already gone to roost on the crosspiece under the flower stand that stood by the south kitchen window. Once during the bitter cold winter Logan had brought him in and put him there, and that had been enough. Tommy considered the flower stand his property. Speckle, his mate, whose feathers were a lacy black and white, roosted in the henhouse with the big chickens. Now Tommy untucked his head from his wing and his small sharp beak reached out to jab Ponto. Then he flew to Logan's shoulder, where the red glints of his feathers were echoed in the boy's curly auburn thatch. He leaned around to peer into Logan's face, and Logan rubbed his chin against him.

When supper was ready, Tommy was entirely willing to

hop to the table and share Logan's meal. Ma could not put up with this, so the bantam retired to his perch, his dignity only slightly ruffled.

The family sat down to the biggest treat they had had for a long time—speckled trout baked in cream! Though fish were not biting in the high muddy water, Ma had managed to snag these. She had bear's cabbage greens, corn pone, and big bowls of clabber to go with them.

"Please pass the sugar," said John, struggling to keep awake long enough to eat.

"John," chided Ma, "you know we haven't any sugar. We don't even have any molasses. We ate it all last winter."

"Pa'll bring some when he comes from Georgetown," said Logan.

" 'T ain't no sugar, take some salt, please," John sighed.

Nobody laughed. John was doing what they had all been doing for the last six years, ever since they had left Sedalia, Missouri, in a wagon train to Colorado: making the best of what they had. There were not many luxuries on the frontier, but, as Pa said, they had so much that little things did not matter. They felt as though they owned all Bear River valley and the mountains around, the creeks, the forests, the fields of dogtooth violets and bluebells.

Actually they did not own a foot of ground. The claim notice Pa had written in a peeled square on an aspen tree when he had discovered this place in 1873 was still plain. He had added on to his original cabin till there were four rooms in the shape of a cross, with a roofed-over court in the middle. The west wing with its crude rock chimney was the kitchen. Pa had hauled in a stove so that cooking no longer had to be done in the fireplace, which Ma now used as a storage space for kettles. The south room, dignified by the Seth Thomas clock on the shelf and by the post office, was the parlor; the east room was the milkhouse and storeroom; while the north room against the hill was the bedroom, though beds overflowed to all parts of the house when travelers stopped. The court in the center, joining the four cabins, served as a large extra room—a place in which to store wagon covers, hides, traps, tools, and whatnot. The dogs slept there. In summer, wide passageways at each corner were open, permitting a cool breeze to blow through, and in winter they were closed with canvas to keep out the snow.

Pa had grubbed away enough sagebrush to plant a garden. He had built a corral. He had made it clear in every possible way that this was his home. But until he had a patent from the United States government, there was no assurance that someone could not take the land away from him. Someday, he said, these mineral springs would be valuable. And so on this trip Outside he was going to Denver to see how he could obtain permanent title to them. This was even more important than bringing in provisions.

John was just salting his clabber, and Logan was sneaking a fish head to Tabby, when Spy dived through the cabin and hid behind the stove. Dick, the young pet woodchuck that had rolled up there for the night, grumbled sleepily.

There was a movement in the open doorway

The candle flame bent in a gust of wind, and there was a movement in the open doorway.

Ma caught up the candle. The yellow flare picked out a face almost hidden in a shrubbery of black whiskers. A voice rumbled, "Howdy, folks!"

"Why, it's Trader Shouse," Ma exclaimed in relief. "Come in, Mr. Shouse!"

He was already in, his Indian moccasins making no sound on the elk-hide rug. If he had straightened up, he might have been as tall as Pa, but he walked with a slouch. "I see you wintered through all right," he said. "I come to let you know I was back."

"And to get a square meal, I bet," Logan muttered under his breath.

In some ways Trader Shouse was like an Indian: he wore a string of beads around his neck and a big silver ring on one forefinger, and he loved to eat. Last summer he had seemed to smell Ma's dried-apple dumplings clear down to his trading post a couple of miles south. The family had been glad when he had left for the winter. Now it had been so long since they had seen anyone besides themselves and occasionally the mail carrier that they were actually glad to have him back.

The trader swung a bulging saddlebag from his shoulder.

Ponto came wagging and sniffing, but Spy, peeking from behind the stove, growled.

"What's the matter with that black dog?"

"She's afraid of Indians," explained Logan, "and you smell like an Ind——"

Hastily Ma broke in, "Sit down and have some supper, Mr. Shouse."

"That's another thing," the trader said. "The Utes are back. Thought I'd better warn you."

A look passed between Lulie and Logan. "The cows must have seen 'em or smelled 'em," said Lulie. "I guess that's why they were so spooky tonight."

"Where's Big Jim?" The trader's eyes, hard and round as chokecherries, pried into the room. Big Jim was what the Indians called Pa.

"Gone Outside for provisions," Ma told him.

John could wait no longer. "What have you got in your sack?" he asked.

"I'll show you, bub!" The trader squatted on his heels to pull things out of the saddlebag. "First, a purty red dress for the mama!"

Ma fingered the bright, new goods. Beside it, the dress she wore looked faded and gray.

"And here's a dandy knife for the boy."

"Gee whillikins!" cried Logan.

"And this for the little feller——"

John clutched the small round looking glass, fascinated by the way he could flash candlelight about the room.

"And here's something Sissy will like."

"My name's not Sissy!" retorted Lulie.

Trader Shouse took from his sack a pair of high blue kid shoes with shiny blue buttons.

"Oh! Oh!" Lulie reached for them. They were the loveliest shoes she had ever seen. Annie, her doll, had blue kid shoes, but these were even prettier than Annie's.

"Try 'em on," urged the trader.

Lulie sat on the floor and kicked off the shapeless homemade moccasins she had had to wear since her shoes had given out. Oh, wonderful! She could thrust her feet into those shoes—no matter how the leather pinched! She pictured herself walking grandly in them.

"What'll you gimme for 'em?"

Because Ma knew what it was to want something pretty, she said gently, "Even if they fit, Lulie, they would only last you about two days. They are not for a mountain girl."

Trader Shouse wiped the back of his hand across his whiskers. "What'll you gimme for the dress goods?"

"We have no money to spend for such as this, nor anything to trade," said Ma. "You had better put all these things back in your bag, Mr. Shouse."

Slowly Lulie took off the shoes. "I had some marten skins——" she stammered. She and her brothers had done a little trapping last winter, and Pa had taken the skins to sell Outside. "Maybe, if you could wait till Pa comes——"

The trader stuffed the shoes into his bag and leaned it by the door. "The Utes are loaded with buckskin," he grunted. "They'll trade with me."

"Anyway, have some supper, Mr. Shouse," said Ma with a sigh.

She heaped a plate, and the man ate ravenously, wiping his hands on his buckskins. Lulie could see why his vest looked the way it did. She could not swallow another bite for thinking of the blue shoes.

The visitor gobbled his corn pone and looked for more.

"You ate the last one!" accused John.

Embarrassed, Ma said, "I used all the corn meal. We're out of most everything."

"But Pa'll bring a wagonload of goodies," John said.

"And that isn't the best," boasted Logan. "He'll have the patent to our land."

"He'll what?" snapped Trader Shouse.

"Oh, son, you shouldn't——"

"Well, that's what he said. So nobody can take it away from us."

"He cain't git a patent! This country ain't even surveyed!" The trader glared about him. "And when it is, I've got first right to these springs!"

A deep, shocked silence met this statement, broken only by the jigging of the teakettle.

Then Ma said, flushing, "We have squatters' rights, Mr. Shouse!"

"Squatters' rights!" The trader jumped to his feet, gesticulating angrily. "Who do you think built that cabin by the cave?"

The cave to which he referred was a hole in the ground

in the middle of a white bench of mineral formation south of the river. Water flowed into its black craw from several nearby springs, and disappeared with deep gurglings. Behind it towered the steep, spruce-covered hill, and below it stretched a marsh of springs.

"There isn't any cabin——" Lulie began, and stopped because she remembered that square of rotting logs and the broken-down stones of a chimney in the edge of the spruces.

"A snowslide smashed it," Trader Shouse said, as if reading her mind, "so I moved down by the Utes's race track where I could trade better. But that was my claim cabin."

He picked up his sack, kicked at Tobe, who spit back at him, and glowered about. "If anybody owns Medicine Springs," he declared, "I do!"

CHAPTER III

"Medicine Springs" was the Indian name for the mineral pools near which Pa had built his cabin. "Steamboat Springs" was the white man's name, and this was rooted in the dim era of the early fur trappers. Pa had learned the tale from some old mountain man—how two French trappers, coming along Bear River for the first time, had heard a chugging sound. Believing they had reached a navigated river, one had exclaimed to the other, "Steamboat, by gar!" They had soon discovered that their find was no steamboat —only a spring, spouting noisily to the south of the river and hurling water like a small geyser.

The name had stuck. The spring continued to chug. Later in the season it could be heard almost to the cabin, but now the roar of the river drowned out every other sound.

The morning after Trader Shouse had made his startling claim, Lulie peered out the window at the valley the Crawfords had come to look upon as their own. Her troubled gaze lingered on the lush, velvety mounds of the mineral springs, some only a few feet from the kitchen door. All the game trails led to them as to a salt lick. Soon the grass fringing them, flavored with minerals, would be trampled and closely cropped. Now it was still fresh and green.

She was thinking what good times she and Logan and John had had playing follow-the-leader among the labyrinth of pools. There were a few solid spots, but most of the knolls were spongy and jiggly. It took expert calculation to jump from mound to mound and not miss their footing. If they slipped, they sometimes sank to their waists. Lulie had discovered the Iron Spring by stepping in it, and now it was everybody's favorite. Ma always insisted they take off their shoes and stockings when they explored the marsh. Then, before they went to bed, she further insisted they scrub the iron-stained mud and the soda-white clay from their feet. John always fell asleep before he could get his feet washed, and Lulie invariably had to finish for him.

The children knew every spring—the little ones that tinkled in their small, rush-grown cups, and the big ones that burbled loudly. All made a kind of friendly conversation. Lulie loved to watch the chains of iridescent bubbles rise to the surface and burst. She and her brothers examined the odd, jointed reeds and grasses and picked the mallows that bloomed in season. They squeezed the green blobs of algae and admired the pink scum on some of the pools. And they considered the inhabitants of the marsh their special friends—the killdeer, frogs, and muskrats; the red-winged blackbirds and shy, long-faced Wilson's snipes; the tiny songsters whose names they did not know.

Lulie thought how dreadful it would be to have to leave all this and move on somewhere else or go back across the endless, dusty plains.

"Wish Pa would come," muttered Logan.

"I look for him today, sure!" Ma had proclaimed every day for two weeks, and the children had nearly worn the roof out, climbing the ladder to the top so they could see farther up the valley. The roof was dirt over pine poles, and the dirt fell through on the inside where they tramped too much. Spy climbed up and down with them, but awkward Ponto could not stick on the ladder.

Every night, when Pa had not come, they reminded themselves it was 150 miles to Georgetown and farther still to Denver, across two mountain ranges, with the road little more than an Indian trail. With creeks over their banks and thousands of little rivers pouring from the snow on the peaks, it was a wonder a man could travel at all, let alone drive a wagon.

There was plenty to see down the valley to the west. Announced by the shrill blasts of woodchucks on the hill, the Utes were returning to their summer hunting grounds. Copper-skinned men on horseback drove herds of ponies to the meadows, while squaws on foot led other ponies dragging tepee poles and packed with skins, blankets, and kettles, on top of which the children clung. One horse dragged a travois on which lay a gaunt Indian man.

Spy skittered into the kitchen to crouch behind the stove, growling.

Yarmonite, the subchief at the head of the Bear River Utes, rode directly to the cabin. Though he had seen many summers, he was not yet an old man, for he sat straight and sturdy on his pony, his thick, moccasined feet braced in stir-rups of bent willows encased in rawhide. He had a square, kindly face.

Ma came out to greet him. For five years the Crawfords and Yarmonite had been summer neighbors. "I'm glad to see you, Yarmonite," she said with genuine warmth, shaking his hand.

One of the chief's eyes was clouded from some injury, but the other, dark and keen, searched beyond Ma through the doorway.

"Big Jim come!" he said with urgency. "My brother Tabby heap sick—mebbeso die."

"Big Jim not here," Ma told him. "Gone to Denver."

The chief's disappointment showed in the heavy way his stocky frame settled back in the narrow Indian saddle deco-rated with rows of brass tacks.

"My prend (friend) gone Denber City," he repeated. Then, as if to himself, "But Medicine Springs here."

He looked toward the pond and across the river where the clear, greenish spring water rushed out of holes in the honeycombed rocks and splashed into the stream. His nos-trils flared with the clean, salty smell of the Big Bubbling Spring. Then he turned and looked at the tall mountains—green near the valley, and higher up shining with new cat-kins on the aspens—as if he were saying "hello" to old friends and remembering that since the beginning of time the Utes had been coming to Medicine Springs so the healing waters could take the aches out of the old and ailing ones.

Yarmonite's pony nipped hungrily at the salty mineral grass. White dust from the lower country matted the pony's mane and tail, dulled the shine of the beads on Yarmonite's buckskins, and powdered the otter fur that bound the ends of his stubby braids. He must have hurried to get here. He must have pushed his band hard, believing Medicine Springs would help Tabby, and recollecting, no doubt, how Pa had saved an Indian's life last year. That Indian had accidentally shot himself in the leg. His friends had come for Pa, crying, "The bleed heap come out!" Pa, who had experienced such things in the war, had applied a tourniquet to stop the bleeding, then tended the wound, and the fellow had got well. The circumstances had been quite different, but nevertheless Yarmonite must have hoped Pa could do something for Tabby.

His gaze returned to the log cabin and Ma in her worn blue apron. "White squaw come!"

Ma did not hesitate. "You stay here," she admonished the children. She looked small and dainty as she followed Yarmonite toward the place where Tabby's squaws were already setting up the pine poles of his lodge and the medicine man was getting ready to build a medicine fire.

Pretty soon Ma returned to the cabin to brew some herb tea.

"Is Tabby very sick, Ma?" asked Lulie.

"Yes, very sick," she said, her face grave. "I wish your Pa was here."

The next day the women of Tabby's lodge made a sweat bath. First they covered a skeleton of poles with blankets and skins, and inside this, they dug a hole in which they built a fire. Then they put stones into the hole, and when the stones were hot, poured cold water on them to make steam. Tabby was laid in the steam, so that the evil would be sweated out of him.

When Tabby was back in his own lodge, the medicine man worked over him many hours. From the tepee came gurgling sounds and high-keyed grunts and now and then a loud howl. But Tabby did not seem to get any better.

Meanwhile, a town of tepees had sprung up on the sagebrush mesa about Soda Creek. There were seventy-five or eighty lodges of red smoked elk hide, fastened to the ground by wooden pegs of chokecherry—each lodge with its smoke flap "ears" that could be adjusted according to the wind. Some of the tepees were decorated with green, blue, and yellow pictures that showed the war records of their owners. The medicine man's tepee was painted with symbols of his medicine.

Last year a happy hubbub had attended the Utes' return to their summer hunting grounds. The squaws had chattered like magpies as they had gathered wood, tended the iron pots swung on poles over the fires, and watched the tall coffeepots that had nothing in them except a lot of water and a few coffee berries floating on top. The men had raced their ponies or sat on their blankets playing games; or scooped the red and yellow color out of the "paint pots" left by the Iron Spring and smeared the good, warm colors on their faces and bodies.

This year the hunters rode out and returned with fat game. The squaws peeled young aspen trees and scraped the sweet inner bark to make a delicate dish for their men. But a certain uneasiness hovered over all. Tabby was sick.

Only the children laughed and enjoyed the glistening springtime. Though the little Indian girls were too timid to come to the cabin unless they were with their mothers, Charlie Yarmonite, the chief's son—a slim, bright-eyed lad of about fourteen—came every day.

Logan was so delighted to have a boy to play with that he could hardly take time to eat. Since last summer he and Charlie had both grown in inches and in experience. They had many things to tell each other. Yarmonite made each of them a bow and some play arrows of sharpened sticks, and the two went hunting chipmunks and woodchucks. Charlie helped bring in the cows and horses, and sometimes the other Indians did, too. The Crawford stock soon became used to the Utes and paid no attention to them. Charlie even played croquet with Lulie, Logan, and John in the level spot between the corral and the Iron Spring.

The cabin had many visitors. They never knocked. Ma and Lulie would look up from sweeping or washing dishes, and there would be an Indian peering through door or window, wanting "beescuit and shug."

The Utes were in no way poor or hungry. They had plenty of blankets, and both men and women wore bracelets, earrings, and finger rings, and all kinds of gewgaws. They owned hundreds of horses. They had all the venison they could eat. And soon the valley would furnish them with an abundance of yampa roots, which the squaws would pound into yellow meal. The river derived its Indian name, Yampa, from these roots, though it was called Bear River by the white men.

Most of the Utes were like children, curious and friendly, and they had a strong sweet tooth. Ma had always had biscuit and sugar to give them before. Now all she had was milk and cheese. The squaws bobbed their heads goodnaturedly when she showed them the empty flour bin and empty sugar bowl. Though the braves scorned milk, saying it was for papooses, Yarmonite's squaw took some in a blackened kettle, and returned with a chunk of venison.

She also had a piece of buckskin from which she set about making moccasins for Ma and Lulie, Logan and John. As she sat on the floor of the kitchen, expertly threading sinews back and forth, her shy dark eyes admired the stove and the rocking chair. When she got up to go, the bead ornaments and bits of brass on her broad leather belt jingled. She could talk little English, and Ma could talk no Ute, but somehow the two managed to "visit."

Yarmonite's squaw carried the moccasins to her tepee to finish. In a day or two she brought them back.

"Why, they're all beaded!" Ma exclaimed. "They're beautiful! I thought only men had beads on their moccasins."

The squaw beamed. She pointed to her own plain toes. "Ute squaw, no," she said. "White squaw, yes."

She had something else to show—a prized possession, for which, she sighed, Yarmonite had paid a good running pony.

Lulie took one agonized look. "Oh!" she wailed. "She's got my blue shoes!"

Though the squaw did not understand the words, she did understand the envy in Lulie's tone. The pleasure faded from her eyes. Quickly she hid the shoes under a fold of her skirt and, backing away, scuttled out the door and up the trail.

"Lulie, Lulie!" Ma was reproving. "I'm afraid you hurt her feelings."

Lulie swallowed hard. "I didn't mean to, Ma," she said in an ashamed voice, "but I've been planning—I hoped maybe when Pa sold my marten skins—— Oh, Ma, she can't begin to get her feet in those shoes!"

"Anyhow, she loves 'em," commented John.

Yarmonite's squaw must have hidden her treasures in her tepee. It would be many days before Lulie would see those blue shoes again.

In the weeks that followed there were things other than

shoes to think about. Most of the Indians did not worry the Crawfords. Only when the paunchy Colorow and his friends came to the cabin was the family uneasy. Colorow was larger than the average Ute, and it was said that he was really an Apache or Comanche who had been stolen by the Utes as a baby. He had offered to trade Ma thirty ponies apiece for Logan and John because they had red hair. He had not offered anything for Lulie because her hair was only very dark brown, and she was glad of it! Wherever Colorow went, Piah went, too. He was younger, his sullen face made startling by stripes of vermilion paint across his cheeks. Last year a white man had been murdered at Cheyenne Wells, and Colorow and Piah were reported to have had a hand in it.

Now, according to Charlie Yarmonite, they and some other braves who had never been on the warpath were getting excited and saying that all the troubles of the Utes were caused by the white people in Ute country—especially by Agent Meeker, who was "heap fool." They had been saying crazy things ever since the Snow Moons, when the annuities from Washington had been late. But Yarmonite and Tabby had talked wisely to them.

Tabby could no longer talk to those braves, and they did not have time to listen to Yarmonite because they were always going down to Trader Shouse's to race their ponies and play games. Trader Shouse had some shiny new Winchester guns that they heap much wanted.

Charlie begged to be allowed to go to the race track, too, but Yarmonite would not let him.

The chief seemed troubled. He and the old ones of his band often came to the Big Bubbling Spring to sit and smoke and stare into its flashing depths. The medicine waters had not healed Tabby, nor had the sweat bath. Not all the medicine man's skill nor the sweet smoke of spruce branches had made him well. Nor had the White Squaw's herbs.

Yarmonite's moccasins seemed weighted with rocks as he padded to the cabin where his squaw was helping Lulie turn the crank of the big square churn. He spoke his thoughts aloud when he said, "Tabby heap good Injun. If he go Happy Hunting Ground, Injuns shootum heap good running horses go with him." He spread eight of his fingers, meaning eight horses.

Ma, who was wiping out the wooden bowl in which to work the butter, shook her head. "Great Spirit not want Indians to kill horses," she told him earnestly, using his own way of speaking. "Mebbeso Tabby's papooses cry for biscuit."

Yarmonite considered. Finally he said, "Sun here"— pointing up to indicate a time about noon—"Injuns come to tepee. I tell what White Squaw say."

As he turned to go, a bunch of braves whipped by on their ponies, making yipping sounds like coyotes. They rode so fast that Lulie might not have recognized Piah if it had not been for the red saddle blanket he always flaunted, and his habit of standing tall in his stirrups while the other Indians lay low along their ponies' necks. Piah and his friends would not be in Yarmonite's tepee to hear what the chief had to say. They were on their way to Trader Shouse's to play games and try to win those shiny new Winchester guns.

CHAPTER IV

Logan and Charlie Yarmonite were going hunting, and since they could outrun John and did not want a "squaw" along, Lulie and John were left to entertain themselves.

"We don't care," said Lulie. "We wouldn't hunt poor little chipmunks anyhow. You call Fleet and Fanny, and I'll get Dick Woodchuck and we'll go down by the Bent Cottonwood and have singing school."

Dick was stretched on a rock behind the cabin, taking his afternoon sunbath. When she picked him up, he scolded her and bit her—not hard, just in play. She tucked him under her arm and went into the bedroom to get Annie, her doll, out of the tray of Ma's tin trunk. Lulie had outgrown dolls, but there were times when she needed an audience. Annie served this purpose well. She was really a beautiful doll. Her black porcelain hair was curly and parted in the middle, her cheeks were pink, and her eyes were blue. She had tiny fingers fashioned of fine leather, and blue kid shoes that seemed to have walked a long distance. She wore a red dress with a fine white sprig in it, of the same material as the lining to Ma's "crazy quilt." On second thought, Lulie also took Annie's hat and her spare dress.

"Here, Fleet! Here, Fanny!" John called.

The fawns bounded out of the willows to see if it was feeding time, and Spy came wagging, too. Ponto had gone with the boys.

There was a squashy wet carpet of buttercups and bluebells all around, but the sand beside the Bent Cottonwood was a playroom, warm and dry. Lightning or heavy snow had broken the immense old tree into the river. The branches still hung there, swayed by the current, and the hollow trunk with its numerous passageways, cracks, and cubbyholes provided a home for some of Dick's cousins.

Mrs. Woodchuck and three young ones who had been taking a nap on their "balcony" popped into a hole when company arrived.

Lulie set Annie on the doll's quilt against a willow clump. "You may have the front seat, Annie," she said.

She put Annie's spare dress on Dick, though he was so fat she could not button it. Then she tried Annie's hat on him. When Dick sat up and scolded, the effect was charming. John laughed and clapped his hands.

Since Dick would not keep the hat on, she tied it on Spy. It took much petting and coaxing to make Spy wear it.

"Now," said Lulie, looking around at her assembled scholars, "is everybody present? I'll play the organ, and you all sing."

"You haven't got any organ," said practical John.

"Maybe Pa'll bring me one if he can sell my marten skins for enough." For a moment Lulie savored the thought. She had taken organ lessons the winter they had spent in Boulder, and she had dreamed of an organ all her own ever since.

"Anyhow, we'll play that this log is an organ," she said, "and this rock is my stool. Now I'll get the song book."

Though the woodchuck family owned most of the Bent Cottonwood, Lulie used one hole for a cupboard. She reached into her cupboard and lifted out the song book Pa had hauled from Georgetown with the provisions last fall.

She gave a dismayed cry. "Oh dear! Oh *dear!* Just look at this!"

"I guess the woodchucks ate it," said John.

"I didn't think they could get into that hole, and I didn't think they'd eat paper!"

Anxiously she examined the small brown book, wider than it was tall, so it would fit easily on an organ rack. It would have been hard to read the title if she had not known that it said *Golden Gateway Hymns,* for the N and S were gnawed away, and the edge of the cardboard cover had bites in it.

"Well, anyway, the inside isn't hurt," she tried to console herself. "The music's all here."

It was no use crying over spilled milk, Ma said. Lulie dusted the book on her skirt and put it on the "organ," propped against a convenient dead stub.

"School will come to order," she announced as she sat down on the imaginary plush-covered stool. "We will sing Number 102."

Pulling out all the stops, she struck a grand chord.

"Amazing grace, how sweet the sound . . ." Her clear

high voice sang the hymn through, the robins and wrens in the willows helping her. John sang all on the same note, and he soon ran out of words. Lulie knew the words by heart. If the woodchucks had eaten the whole book, she would still have been able to remember most of it because the family had sung everything in it over and over again during the winter.

Pa had known other songs to teach them, also. He had a fine baritone voice and had been taught by his father, who had conducted a neighborhood singing school in Missouri. Logan and Lulie shared Pa's love of singing. Pa's favorites were the old Scottish ballads, including "Scots Wha Hae Wi' Wallace Bled." Logan's choice was "The Hunters of Kentucky." Lulie preferred pieces like "Come Where the Lilies Bloom," because she could sing the top part while Pa came booming in with the bass notes. Ma followed along with her small sweet voice, and John warbled to suit himself.

Lulie could have spent the entire afternoon singing, but noting that her scholars' interest was lagging, she closed the book.

"We will now have arithmetic," she announced. "Master John, how many water ouzels do you see?"

A pair of the pudgy, slate-gray birds were building a nest behind a waterfall that cascaded from a spring across the river. John had been watching them dart in and out through the spray without getting a feather wet.

"Four," he said.

The teacher rapped for attention. "I'm afraid you don't know your numbers, Master John. Tell me, how many legs has a chicken?"

"Four," maintained the student.

"That's silly," exclaimed the teacher. "You may be excused to go home and find a chicken and count its legs!"

Obediently John scrambled to his feet and trotted toward the cabin. Spy finished pawing off her bonnet to run with him. Dick was trying to chew his way out of his dress. To keep him from spoiling it, Lulie took it off, whereupon he climbed the Bent Cottonwood with many grunts and grumbles. Fleet and Fanny wandered away. The only scholar left was Annie, who sat staring patiently ahead of her.

"We will sing another song and be dismissed," said the teacher, thumbing through the book for the number.

Suddenly Dick's grumbling changed to sharp warning as a shadow fell across the sand. Lulie whirled from the organ to see an Indian standing there. She recognized Piah, the sullen-faced Ute who had ridden off with Colorow this morning. Her heart gave a thump.

She stammered, "H-hello!"

Piah's expression was unusually glum. Since he was afoot, Lulie guessed it had been an unlucky day for him at Trader Shouse's race track.

"Unh," said Piah, his black eyes fastening on Annie. He took a stumbling step toward the doll, and this was strange because Indians were usually as sure-footed as cats. A queer, sweetish smell hung about him. He snatched Annie by her

A shadow fell across the sand

neck, whipped out his knife, and went through the motions of scalping her before her startled mother and teacher could do more than gasp.

Then he flung her in a beaver hole and stood staring about him, that queer glitter in his eyes. No telling what might have happened next if Dick's kinfolks on the point of hill above the Iron Spring had not whistled that someone was coming.

Piah melted into the willows.

Lulie picked poor Annie out of the mud and ran to the cabin as fast as she could.

CHAPTER V

Lulie was relieved to recognize Ellis Clark, a young man who carried mail between Steamboat Springs and Hayden, twenty-five miles down the river. He was walking and leading his long-legged sorrel, which he called Blaze because of a white streak on its nose. He always hallooed when he came in sight, and the first one to reach him was privileged to ride to the cabin. This was considered a treat, since Blaze could gallop faster than any of the fat Crawford horses. Riding him was almost like flying. The Indians all wanted that horse. They thought it was a shame to waste a good running horse on carrying mail, but Ellis was not interested in swapping or racing.

Ma, sleeves above her elbows and broom still in hand, hurried to the white mineral hill by the Warm Iron Spring to meet him.

Logan ran, shouting, "Did you bring me a letter?"

John reached Blaze first and climbed to the saddle. Ordinarily Lulie would have been ahead of them all, but her legs felt wobbly after her encounter with Piah. Anyhow, Blaze was not galloping today. He was walking with a limp.

"What's the matter with Blaze?" were Ma's first words.

"Sprained his shoulder swimming Elk River last trip

34

down," said Ellis. "It doesn't bother him unless he's tired." He jerked his head toward the town of tepees. "I see your neighbors are back."

"Yes," said Ma. "Do you have some letters for us?"

Ellis laughed. He had a nice laugh. "Yes, *ma'am!*" he said, untying the mail sack from behind the saddle.

They all followed him into the cabin, and Ma reached the key from its nail beside the "Post Office," which was a box that had once held dried peaches and which Pa had nailed to the wall and partitioned into cubbyholes, labeling them *Letters Received, Letters to Mail, Stamps.*

Mail service to Bear River valley had been established less than a year. How well Lulie remembered seeing tall, raw-boned Mann Redmond from Middle Park ride into Steamboat Springs last summer with the first mail sack. He had handed Pa the key. Inside the sack had been a few supplies and Pa's commission as postmaster. The mail was carried from Georgetown to Hot Sulphur Springs by stage, and from there it was packed on horseback over Gore Range and by way of Morrison Creek trail to Steamboat Springs and as far as Hayden.

The mail from Outside was the most exciting because it nearly always brought a letter from kinfolks in Missouri. The mail from Hayden was never very newsy since there were only three families in that part of the valley, and they hadn't much to write about. But they always made a point of writing something, and Ma always sent a note to them.

"Here's a letter from Mrs. Smart to me," Ma said, "and

here's one for you, Lulie—— Goodness, what happened to Annie?"

Lulie was trying to wring the water out of Annie's clothes. "Piah," she said.

"Piah!"

"I was having school, and he came and tried to scalp her, and then he threw her in a beaver hole and went away." With the hem of her dress Lulie wiped Annie's face. "Don't you care," she comforted. "He didn't get a lock of your beautiful hair, for it's tight to your head."

The letter lay unopened in Ma's hand. She said, "Oh, I guess he was just playing."

"He acted queer. And his breath smelled funny."

A look passed between Ma and Ellis Clark.

"Whisky!" Ellis snorted. "The Indians have been gittin' it somewhere. Scairt a woman over on Snake River——" He stopped. "I don't like it."

Ma did not know she was crumpling Mrs. Smart's letter. "The Indians have never troubled us," she said.

"I don't want to scare you," Ellis went on, "but things are different this year. Agent Meeker has plowed up the Utes' race track, and he's tryin' to make them work and build houses and raise gardens. They're born hunters. They don't take to civilization. They're gittin' restless, and anything's liable to touch 'em off."

He nodded toward Tabby's lodge where the medicine song had started again. "What's goin' on yonder?"

"Tabby's very sick," Ma told him.

"If I know Indians, they're liable to blame the whites for that." The frown deepened on Ellis's forehead. "Mr. Crawford's about due, ain't he?"

"I'm expecting him any time," said Ma.

"That's good," muttered Ellis. "Well, I'll unsaddle and picket Blaze."

The mail carriers usually slept in Uncle Henry's cabin, but Ellis brought his blankets and put them in the courtway of Pa's cabin. When Lulie went to bed, he was still sitting in the doorway, smoking.

Sometime in the night Lulie sat bolt upright, startled from her sleep by hideous noises, worse than any howls ever made by coyotes or wolves.

Ma was sitting up in bed, too, listening. "I'm afraid Tabby's gone to the Happy Hunting Ground," she said in a low voice. "Must be his squaws mourning for him."

There was a whining and scratching at the door. Ma got up and let Spy in. The little dog sprang to the bed, scuttling under the covers like a cold wind.

For hours, Lulie thought, the screeching and wailing continued. Above it all a robin started his dawn song. As it began to be light, the cabin jarred with the thud of horses' hoofs going past the door and down the trail. They kept coming, like the long rumble of thunder. There must have been a lot of horses. Ma and Lulie huddled, listening. Through the window they could make out a dark cavalcade moving steadily by. At last the hoofbeats were swallowed in the rush of creek and river, and the loud joyous singing of birds in the willows.

When the sun came up, Tabby's lodge was no longer there, and not a tepee remained on the mesa above Soda Creek.

Ma built the fire in the stove. Ellis came stomping up the trail. He looked as though he had not slept all night.

"They're gone," he growled, "lock, stock, and barrel—and so is Blaze!"

CHAPTER VI

Lulie, Ma, and Ellis Clark stood shivering in the dooryard that sharp June dawn after Tabby died; they peered at the valley, empty except for the drifting smoke from old campfires and the dark trails in the dew of the grass where the Utes had fled.

"Looks like them Indians took Blaze!" Ellis exclaimed indignantly.

"Maybe he just got scared at the noise and pulled his picket pin," chattered Lulie.

"Mebbe."

"I don't see our horses either," said Ma. "Usually they're right up the gulch. Thank goodness the cows are still in the corral."

She waked the boys to help with the milking. "Hurry," she said, "we must do the chores and then go hunt the horses."

Logan and John, who had not heard any of the commotion, came stumbling to breakfast, half asleep, but their eyes popped wide open when they heard what had happened in the night.

"Why did the Indians all go away?" cried John.

"They never stay where someone has died," Ellis grunted. "Won't even eat there."

"Will they ever come back?" Logan could not believe that his friend, Charlie Yarmonite, would leave without telling him.

"Oh, sure. When they git poor old Tabby hid away in some cave or crevice, they'll make another camp and be hanging around your cabin, same as usual."

"Tabby was a good Indian," Ma said. "He could help Yarmonite control some of those renegades. Now, I wonder . . ."

*

The valley was so trampled it was almost impossible to read sign. There were no horses up the gulch or around the hill or near the Bath Spring. Finally Ellis discovered shod tracks leading up Soda Creek. Following these, he and Lulie and Logan at last came upon the Crawford horses in a willow basin a couple of miles from home.

"Blaze ain't here," Ellis said, disappointed. "Thought maybe he'd got with your herd."

Tired and hungry, they each caught a mount and rode back home, driving the other horses before them. As they came in sight of the cabin, they saw a pony grazing by the Iron Spring.

"There he is!" cried Lulie.

"That ain't Blaze!" Ellis said, disgusted.

On second look Lulie could see that the horse by the Iron Spring was no graceful long-legged sorrel, but a poddy bay with his forelock in his eyes and a scraggly mane. He turned a pair of vicious hoofs when Ponto raced up to investigate.

The owner of the strange horse, a gnarly pine knot of an old man, perched on the bench by the cabin, talking to Ma and John. He wore a hat, weathered and shapeless, and a ragged wool shirt, threadbare but clean. His lean chin was sparsely frosted with whiskers.

He chuckled a greeting. "Howdy!"

"Why, it's Uncle Tow!" shouted Logan, skinning off his horse and running up to the visitor. "Where've you been all winter, Uncle Tow?"

"In my 'hole,' " said the old man. "Me and Podge."

Lulie knew that in mountain language a "hole" was a sheltered valley where snow never got too deep for a horse to feed. The snow was four to six feet deep most places in the Rockies.

Ellis shook hands with the visitor. "Howdy, Uncle Tow. How's your placer claim?"

Uncle Tow held up a buckskin bag heavy with something. "I got enough to buy some beans and some more salt," he stated, a sparkle in his blue eyes, "and have a leetle fun. I come down to palaver with the Utes and play some games mebbe. But"—he finished with childish disappointment—"they ain't here."

"I told him about Tabby," said Ma.

"I seen a bunch headin' up Elk River with a big buckskin bundle on a pony. Knowed they was on a buryin' trip, so I set on the hill and let 'em go by. Was hopin' we could run some races mebbe. After all winter alone, a feller likes to have some fun. Ain't that so, Podge?" He got up and walked over to the horse.

Podge quit gorging himself long enough to lay back his ears and bare yellow teeth at his owner.

The old man grinned. "He's got spirit, that hoss. And he can travel, too, when he's a mind."

"You didn't see a blaze-faced sorrel runnin' loose anywhere, did you?" inquired Ellis.

"The Injuns had some hosses, but I don't think there was any sorrels. I figured they was goin' to send them to the Happy Hunting Ground with the pore feller in the bundle."

Ellis looked glum.

While Ma and Lulie prepared dinner, Uncle Tow squatted on his heels in the shade, whittling slivers of jerky from a worn chunk he produced from his pack and feeding them alternately to himself and John, who squatted beside him. Dick Woodchuck examined the stranger's pockets, and when he found nothing to interest him, sat up with his paws across his fat stomach and scolded. Tommy Bantam, always curious about everything, perched on Uncle Tow's shoulder, his head on one side, listening to the old man's creaky voice. Spy, usually so shy, lay asleep at his feet.

Trader Shouse came riding up the valley to find out what had become of his customers, the Utes, and also to learn

whether Pa had returned. At first he was surly when he saw
Uncle Tow. "Wal," he grumbled, "I come up lookin' for
the Injuns, and all I find is a runt of a prospector."

However, when he saw the bag of gold dust and the cross-
fox fur that Uncle Tow had in his pack, he suddenly cheered
up. "How about playin' a game with me?" he offered.

"I'll go you!" said Uncle Tow.

Ellis frowned. "You better let Mrs. Crawford take care of
that gold dust," he suggested.

But after dinner Uncle Tow, trustful as John and excited
at having human companionship once more, went off with
Trader Shouse. "A man's got to have some fun," he said.
"He's goin' to show me a game called 'Canute.' "

The trader, an arm about the old man's shoulders, shuffled
off to find a dry sunny spot.

"Shouse'll clean him, sure," muttered Ellis, as he struck
out on horseback to continue his search for Blaze. Logan
and Spy went with him. Lazy Ponto was taking a nap in the
dusty hollow of the trail.

Ma sent Lulie to the hill with a bucket and a knife to
gather bear's cabbage for supper. The bucket was big and
the greens were small, and Lulie thought she would never
get a mess. She was tired, anyway, from hunting the horses.
She sat down on a rock to rest.

She could see Uncle Tow and the trader engrossed in
their game. They had made several little hills of river sand.
It appeared that one man would bury a stick in a hill while
the other would guess which hill it was in. Seemed as

though the trader always guessed the right one and Uncle Tow never did.

"I don't call that any fun!" she said to herself.

With a sigh she picked up her pail. Her eye caught a movement across the river. A cow elk that had been feeding in the grassy bottom suddenly plunged into the trees. Lulie looked to see what had startled it. The next instant she was running as fast as that elk, shouting, "It's Pa! Pa's home!"

CHAPTER VII

On the far bank stood a tall, familiar figure, vigorously waving his hat. Pa had been gone a month. He had traveled 400 miles, round trip, over the Continental Divide and over the Gore Range; through forests and valleys where his was the first wagon track this spring. Now he was home!

Yet not quite home, for between him and the cabin roared the deep, angry current of Bear River. Ma, Lulie, and John stood on the north bank and shouted to him on the south bank, and his shout came back—a whisper above the water. Ponto ran up and down barking, while Uncle Tow and Trader Shouse quit their game of Canute to join the excitement.

"There's Dave, too!" shrilled John. "Hello, Dave!"

The Negro boy waved the mail sack. Though he had been only as far as Rock Creek, he must have caught up with Pa where the horse trail joined the "road."

Ma hung on to John's galluses. "Oh, I hope they don't try to cross till the water goes down!"

When streams were at flood, travelers in the mountains always made a point of fording in the early morning. The waters were lowest then because the night coolness had retarded snow-melting. Here it was midafternoon, and Pa was not going to wait. He was motioning to Trader Shouse and Uncle Tow.

"Bring the boat!" he yelled.

The boat was a small, stubby wooden shell that Pa had hauled in for just such an emergency. It lay on the bank where the overflow could not reach it.

"What's he think we are—crazy?" growled Trader Shouse.

Uncle Tow studied the river with screwed-up face. "Mebbe he's brought some tobaccy," he ventured. Settling his hat firmly, he picked up the pine pole that served as an oar. "I run out of smokin' tobaccy in February," he remarked as he shoved the boat into the water and leaped in.

The current caught the small craft like a leaf, whirling it around and down. Crouched in the bottom, Uncle Tow poled furiously. He was small but wiry. He managed to reach shore a long way from where he had embarked.

When he had recovered his breath, he and Pa and Dave started back. Since the boat was heavier with three in it, the navigators grounded it within a short distance and came squishing through the marsh made by the overflow—Dave copying Pa's stride, Uncle Tow hopping from hummock to hummock. Pa carried a poke of something under his arm, and Dave had the mail sack.

Though Pa looked tired and whiskery, his blue eyes were eager as a boy's. He threw down the poke and reached for his family with hungry arms.

Ponto jumped joyously on him and Dave.

"Good-fer-nuthin' yaller dawg," crooned Dave, tousling him.

"Where's Logan?" were Pa's first words.

"Gone with Ellis Clark——" Ma began.

". . . to hunt Blaze," said Lulie.

"The Indians came and went away again and Blaze is lost," shouted John on one breath.

Ma clung to Pa, scolding, "Jimmy, the river was too high. You shouldn't have tried——"

"Had to see what's in the mail sack, Maggie." There was booming excitement in Pa's voice. "I'm expecting something important."

"What, Pa?" cried Lulie.

Pa's eyes rested upon the flag, upon the cabin against the hill, and the sunny peace of the valley. "Thought I'd never make it," he muttered. "Gumbo mud two feet deep, and water everywhere."

"Did you get our claim fixed?" piped John.

Pa caught his youngest and swung him high till John's red forelock stood up like a feather. "Yessireebobtail Peter horsefly!" he assured him. "I got things started. The surveyors'll be here in a few weeks."

"Surveyors!" snorted Trader Shouse, without greeting.

"Why, howdy, Mr. Shouse," Pa said. "Yes, that will be a great day for the valley."

"I was here before you!" whined the trader. "I got first right to these springs!"

Pa gave him a level look. "I've no way of knowing," he

said crisply, "but we've been *living* here, and we expect to keep on living here. There's room enough for us all, Shouse, and the survey will help everybody."

Picking up his poke, Pa started for the cabin.

"Now let's get that mail sack open."

"Hey, Dave, I'll help you carry the mail," volunteered John. "Did you bring me a letter?"

"And did you bring me one, Dave?" asked Ma.

"I 'spec's so, Miss Maggie!" Dave's square black face glistened with importance. "Dey's sho' 'nuff somepin' in dis yere bag!"

A minute later he laid the faded canvas pouch on the table in the front room of the cabin.

"It's almost open without being unlocked," observed Lulie. "If that slit were a little bigger . . ."

The sack had been worn and cracked from years of exposure on some other postal route. Though most mail sacks were made of leather, in the mountains, where they often had to be carried on a man's back, they were of lighter material such as canvas. Generally papers and magazines were in a separate bag, but mail to the thinly populated Bear River country was so scanty, it was all put in the same sack.

Snatching the key from its nail, Pa turned it in the lock and dumped the mail onto the table. Quickly he sorted through the letters while everybody crowded around.

"Any mail for me?" asked Trader Shouse.

Uncle Tow did not ask. There was never anything for him.

"Letter for you, Maggie," Pa said, "and one for you, Lulie." He set aside a small packet for Hayden. "Here's Logan's *Youth's Companion* and John's *Chatterbox*, and the *Rocky Mountain News*."

He frowned. He went through everything again, more carefully, turning the sack upside down and shaking it. "It's not here," he muttered.

"What?" inquired Ma.

"Oh—a letter. Reckon it'll be in the next mail."

Pa tried not to show his disappointment. He carried his poke into the kitchen. "Here's a little flour and sugar, Maggie," he said. "Soon as I can ford the wagon you'll have more."

Supper that night was wonderful, in spite of Trader Shouse glowering into his plate; in spite of Uncle Tow peering sadly through the window at Podge, who stood in the dooryard, one leg slumped in boredom.

By all the rules of Canute, Podge was now the property of Trader Shouse. The sack of gold dust and the cross-fox fur also belonged to Trader Shouse, but Uncle Tow appeared to give them little thought. "I'll git you back, Podge," he whispered as he sopped his biscuit in Ma's good gravy. "Don't you worry."

Ellis Clark was out of sorts, too. He and Logan had failed to find any trace of Blaze.

But Lulie, Logan, and John found everything right with the world. Pa was home!

"Pass the sugar, please," said John with satisfaction.

"We shot eighteen grouse, Ma and I," boasted Logan, "and we ate a woodchuck. It was good."

"Speckle is setting," said Lulie. "And I practiced the organ every day so when I get the real organ, I'll remember how to play it. Oh, Pa, did you sell my marten skins, and how much did they bring?"

Pa looked uncomfortable. "I'm sorry to tell you children I had to borrow your money to help buy provisions. But you shall each have any calf you want for your very own, and next year when we drive cattle to market, they should bring a good price."

"Whee-ee!" exclaimed Logan. " 'Druther have a calf anyhow. I'm goin' to take the one with the little white heart on its forehead. Which one you goin' to take, John?"

John considered. "The freckled one, I think."

Lulie stared down at her plate. Next year—an eternity! She had planned on those marten skins to make part payment on an organ. She had hoped—oh, how she had hoped —Pa could haul in that organ on his next trip, as soon as the mud dried.

Then she looked up and noted the tired droop to Pa's shoulders. "I don't mind, Pa," she managed. "I—guess I wouldn't have time to play the organ anyhow."

"Couldn't even fetch shoes or clothes this time." Pa sighed. "Just brought the necessaries. I'll have to go out again soon and take some venison to trade."

"Where is Spy?" asked Ma.

"She stayed down at the corral." Logan looked pointedly at Trader Shouse. "She doesn't like too much company."

At last supper was finished, and Ellis got up. "Well, I'll go hit the hay."

"Me too," yawned Dave.

"Hold on a minute, Dave," Pa said. "You'll want to get an early start tomorrow while the river's down, and I've something to tell you."

Pa waited till Uncle Tow and Trader Shouse went out. The trader caught Podge's lead rope, mounted his own horse, and started back to his camp. Uncle Tow looked wistfully after him, then stumbled across the footlog with Ellis to Uncle Henry's cabin.

Pa shut the door. Lulie knew now the family would hear what he had been bursting to tell. Logan had worked so hard hunting Blaze he had not been able to keep awake, and John was curled asleep on the floor with Ponto, but Lulie and Ma were all ears, and Tommy Bantam kept a golden eye on Pa.

"Dave," Pa proclaimed, "there's going to be an important letter in the mail, probably this trip. I'm trusting you to bring it safely."

"Yassuh!" said Dave.

"It'll have money in it."

"Don't you worry, Mistah Jim. I'll fetch it."

"Who in the world would be sending us money?" Ma wanted to know.

"Uncle Hammond in Missouri. He always insisted if we

The trader started back to his camp

ever needed help to come to him. So I wired him. We have to advance twelve hundred dollars to pay for the survey."

"Twelve hundred dollars!" gasped Ma.

Pa nodded. "You see, Maggie, a whole township has to be surveyed before we can file our claim, and we have to advance the money to the government to make the survey. Afterward, they'll apply it on purchase of our claim.

"It would have been such a simple matter," Pa went on, "but you know Uncle Hammond. He's an old man, and dead set against anything new-fangled or that he doesn't understand. And he doesn't understand about telegraphing money. So"—Pa looked provoked and amused at the same time—"he wired back that he was sending the money by registered mail here to Steamboat Springs."

"Land sakes!" Ma said weakly.

"I know it," Pa agreed. "He doesn't realize all the distance and mountains."

"What if something should happen to it?" worried Lulie. "What if it shouldn't get here?"

"Oh, the mail always gets here sooner or later. And this is registered. I've no doubt it's as safe as can be. The land office has agreed to protect our rights until I can send the money back with the surveyors. The old clerk didn't want to. Said the law stated he had to have the deposit first, but Fred Ingersoll, the surveyor, talked him into it. Fred's a mighty nice young fellow. He and his crew'll be here after he gets a couple of other jobs done in Middle Park."

"Well, I'll be goin' over to the cabin," said Dave.

Before he could stretch to his feet, Tommy Bantam gave a sharp warning note. There was a sudden scratching in the chimney, and amid a cloud of soot something thumped into the fireplace, scattering the kettles Ma had stored there with a clang that sent Ponto leaping aside and woke John and Logan.

"What the devil!" Pa automatically grabbed for a club of stove wood.

Lulie had never heard Pa say that before. Her amazement was divided between Pa and the apparition, which had two gleaming eyes and a tail and scuttled behind the woodbox with a yelp.

"Why, it's Spy!" exclaimed Ma. "Come down the chimney!"

Dave's eyes popped. "Come down the chimbley," he echoed. "That's what she done!"

"Why'd she do that?" cried Lulie. "Here, Spy! Come, Spy!"

The little dog scrooched into the farthest corner, whimpering.

"A good thing we don't keep fire in that fireplace any more," said Ma.

Logan crawled behind the woodbox. "It's just me, Spy. Did you hurt yourself? Whyn't you scratch at the door if you wanted in?"

"Maybe there was something in her way," suggested Lulie, "and she was so scared she had to get in somehow, so she climbed the ladder and jumped down the chimney."

Pa flung open the door. The roar of creek and river rushed into the room. There was no other sound, and there was nothing to be seen in the moonlight that lay over yard and hill.

He stepped into the night, still carrying his firewood. Pretty soon he came back. "There's nothing out there now," he said. "Spy's a funny little dog—easily excited. Reckon she got scared at a prowling fox or bobcat."

But Lulie knew Spy was not afraid of foxes or bobcats!

CHAPTER VIII

Tommy Bantam had just announced dawn with a shrill trumpet from the flower stand when Lulie heard Pa building a fire in the stove, and pretty soon smelled coffee. She jumped out of bed, remembering that this was the day Dave was going to Rock Creek and would probably bring Uncle Hammond's money back in the mail, and shivering in the frosty air, dressed as fast as she could, ran through the center court, and stepped into the warmth of the kitchen.

Dave, Ellis, Uncle Tow, and Pa were seated at the table eating fried grouse, biscuits and gravy by candlelight. Ellis and Uncle Tow ate methodically, but Dave snatched at his food.

"Eat plenty, Dave," Pa advised. "It's a long way to Rock Creek."

"Ain't hongry," Dave said. Gulping down his coffee, he hoisted to his feet and picked up the lunch Ma had fixed for him. As he reached for the mailbag, his six-shooter thumped against the table.

"Jimmy," Ma said anxiously, "hadn't you better go with Dave?"

"No need," Pa said, "and there's too much to do here.

I'll take him over in the boat and help him saddle Coaly, and then I've got to go kill a deer."

From the door Lulie watched Pa and Dave cross the footlog and disappear in the smudgy gray of the willows. Spy limped after them. Lulie wished the little dog could talk and tell what had scared her last night.

"I'll push off, too," Ellis said. "Have to borrow one of your hosses till I can find Blaze."

He stood a moment in the trail, peering at the daylight that was beginning to streak through Fish Creek canyon. Though he must have known something unusual was in the wind, he had a fine way of minding his own business.

"I'll go see how Podge is gittin' on," muttered Uncle Tow, and struck out afoot for Trader Shouse's camp.

*

When Pa poled the boat back, he brought more provisions from the wagon. Lulie was at the riverbank to help him carry them to the cabin.

"Pa," she panted, trotting to keep up, "Trader Shouse said he had first right to these springs, but he hasn't, has he?"

Pa walked the footlog across Soda Creek and eased a sack of flour from his shoulder before he answered, "I don't think so. He's just waked up to the fact that these springs will be valuable someday."

"He says he was here first," said Lulie with a shiver. "He

says that old cabin across the river in the pine grove was his claim cabin."

Pa frowned. "He could make trouble, but once we get our patent there'll be no question."

"I wish the surveyors would hurry!" said Lulie.

With Pa to help, the milking was done in no time. The dew was not even dry on the grass when he turned the cows out to pasture and started up the gulch with his gun to kill a deer.

Though the boys wanted to go with him, they knew it was no use trying to keep up with his long legs. All they could do was stand on a rock and watch him out of sight. They had a double reason for wanting to go with Pa. Ma was taking down the wash boiler from the nail on the outside of the kitchen, and when Ma washed, she put everybody to work.

"Logan," she said briskly, "I wish you'd stir up the fire, and John, bring in more wood. Lulie, you fill the boiler."

"Well, anyhow"—Logan sighed—"maybe we can hear him shoot."

It took buckets and buckets of water to fill that boiler. Lulie, scrambling up and down the trail to Soda Creek, looked across at the pine grove where the old cabin was and could not help feeling uneasy.

In summer the washing was done outdoors away from the heat of the stove. The tubs were set on a bench by the kitchen door, where the hot soapy smell mingled with the perfume of the primroses that grew thick on the hill back of the cabin. As soon as the sun hit the primroses they turned pink—as pink as Ma's face when she bent over the washboard.

Ma rubbed and rubbed Pa's travel-grimed clothes with the cake of homemade soap while the children took turns stirring and "punching" them in the rinse water with a smooth stick.

They all listened for a shot. There was game in every thicket, and Pa seldom had to go far.

"I don't hear anything," said John.

"No, but here come some Indians," said Logan, leaning on his stick.

There had not been an Indian around since Tabby had died. Lulie watched curiously as the handful of squaws and children trudged up the trail, pausing often, almost as if they were afraid. Usually Indians wore their hair braided, though some squaws left theirs loose and were always shaking it out of their eyes. These Indians did not have any front hair to braid or shake. It was cut short from ear to ear. The coarse, ragged ends, framing faces smeared with ashes, made them look like wild creatures. They began a squeaky singsong: "Beescuit! Beescuit!"

"I think that's Tabby's family," said Ma, "and cutting their hair must be a sign of mourning. Poor things!"

She spread biscuits generously with butter and sugar and divided them among the mourners, who squatted in the shade of the cabin.

When Tabby's family had eaten every crumb, they licked

the sugar from their lips and straggled back to the new camp, which they explained by grunts and signs was just below the island. They were careful not to go near the dried willows of Tabby's sweat bath or the mashed-down spot in the grass where his tepee had stood.

By and by Yarmonite came riding up the trail. Though he also took pains to avoid the place where Tabby's tepee had been, he paused to stare into the Big Bubbling Spring before he turned toward the cabin. The chief still wore his braids, but today there were no beads in them—not even a strip of fur. He sat in his saddle heavily while his pony stretched its neck toward the mineral grass.

Ma looked up from her washtub to his square, troubled face. "I'm sorry as can be about Tabby," she told him.

"Me heap poor," Yarmonite muttered. "Give my beads to Tabby to wrap his hair." After a moment he went on, "Utes kill two heap good running horses and one *hea-ea-eap* old pony."

"Why did you do that?" cried John.

"So Tabby have horses to ride in Happy Hunting Ground," Yarmonite answered.

At that moment a shot popped through the stillness.

"There!" yelped Logan. "Pa's got his deer. Come on, John!"

Abandoning the washtubs, they raced up the hill.

Yarmonite's eye caught the imprint of Pa's big foot in the dust. "Sah*wah*waretz!" he exclaimed, and with that word his spirit seemed to revive.

Sahwahwaretz was a name the Utes sometimes gave Pa. It meant "Heap Walk." They could never get over the fact that Pa walked as often as he rode. Ute men never walked if they could help it. Some of them even fished from horseback and threw the fish to their squaws, who took them off the hooks and put on more bait.

"Yes," said Ma, "Sahwahwaretz—Big Jim—is home."

With a nudge of his moccasins, Yarmonite sent his pony up the hill, following Pa's tracks.

A short time later he and Pa and Logan and John returned with the deer across Yarmonite's pony. The chief had saved Pa the trouble of catching a horse.

When the deer had been hung on a hook on the back of the cabin to cool, Indian and white man squatted on their heels in the shade to rest. They had not seen each other since October. Last spring they had had many things to talk about, and had sat together a long time, now and then drawing a picture in the smooth dirt to fill in for their lack of words. Today Yarmonite crouched in silence.

Lulie, taking the clothes off the line, overheard Pa try to renew the old easy understanding between them. Pa said, "The winter was long and cold, but the good summertime is here again, and there are many deer tracks."

Yarmonite took his pipe out of his shirt gravely. Its red stone bowl was fitted with a long reed mouthpiece, decorated with feathers. He stuffed the bowl with dried shreds of kinnikinnick from a small buckskin sack, took an ember from the stove to light it, and sat down cross-legged. When he had drawn on the pipe enough to bring a glow to the kinnikinnick, he pointed the stem to each of the four points of the compass and to the sky and earth. Then he took three long whiffs and passed the pipe to Pa, who also drew on it strongly three times before passing it back.

Pa had smoked with the Utes before. He had sat with them in a solemn circle around their council fire. Lulie remembered his saying, "I hated to put that pipe in my mouth after a dozen Indians had had it in theirs, but I had to!" This time there was only two of them. Yarmonite was deeply in earnest. He had blended his breath with the smoke and given it to the cardinal points and to earth and sky, and so had Pa. Now they were ready to talk.

"Snow gone from ground," Yarmonite said, "but snow still here." He tapped his chest. "Bad medicine in Ute country."

"I'm mighty sorry about Tabby," Pa told him.

"Tabby good Injun. Something make bad medicine." Yarmonite was silent a moment before he abruptly demanded, "What Washington say? What paper man say?"

"The papers say some of the Utes are causing trouble," Pa told him reluctantly. "They say the Utes do not do what Agent Meeker wants."

"Agent Meeker heap fool. Say Injun must make potato, cabbage. Must work. Injun heap lazy. No work. Injun hunt, fish."

"I think Meeker means well," Pa began. "He just doesn't——"

"Meeker bad medicine," Yarmonite declared. "Mebbeso Big Jim take his squaw and papooses, and Yarmonite take his squaw and papooses and go Denber City."

Lulie was puzzled. After Yarmonite's pony had plodded down the trail with the chief humped upon him, Lulie asked, "Pa, why would Yarmonite want us to go to Denver?"

Pa, thoughtfully stroking his skinning knife on the whetrock, muttered, "I don't know, unless——"

"Unless what, Pa?"

". . . there's some kind of trouble in the wind."

CHAPTER IX

If trouble was in the wind, there was no sign of it next morning around the Crawford cabin. As Pa dressed out the deer, he sang:

> "Flow gently, sweet Afton,
>   Amang thy green braes . . ."

There was nothing gentle about the streams in Steamboat Springs. Soda Creek came riproaring from the mountains white with foam, and Bear River thundered over its banks. And there was nothing gentle about Pa's voice. It boomed through the valley till the cows rolled slick eyes at him, the pet fawns hid in the willows, and a killdeer rose from the rushes with a startled screech.

Pa laughed. He took a deep breath of the tangy mineral air. "Dave should get in with the mail tonight," he said.

"And he'll be bringing you-know-what, we hope!" exclaimed Lulie, watching Pa's keen knife lay back the satiny white skin of the deer.

Tobe and Tabby, the big gray cats, sat at a polite distance, washing their faces. Spy lay in the sun, feigning sleep. But Ponto, John, and Logan crowded so close Pa had to say, "Take care!"

Pa worked with the meat all morning. Some of it would

keep a long time hung in the shade on the back of the cabin and still protected by the hide. He cut some of it into steaks and roasts for Ma to use right away. These he put in pans in the milkhouse and tied the pans inside flour sacks. The thick log walls and dirt-covered roof kept the milkhouse as cool as could be. He cut the rest of the meat into long strips and rubbed them with salt. He put these in a large earthenware jar where they would soon make their own brine. After a few days he would take them out, put a string through one end, and hang them in the sun to dry. They did not have to dry clear through. Once the outside was sealed, they would keep any length of time. Pa called the meat thus treated "jerky." Sometimes he smoked it a little with smoke from scrub-oak wood. Sliced and broiled, or whittled into thin pieces and cooked in gravy, it made a welcome variety from common fare. Or eaten just the way it was—half dried and salty—it was oh, so good!

Lulie liked nothing better than to curl up with a story book and read while she nibbled jerky. But the venison Pa was fixing would have to dry a week or two before it would be ready, and right now she had nothing to read. Though the miners from Hahn's Peak sometimes brought her books, no one had been down from the Peak for a long while. Anyhow, she had no heart for reading today. She kept thinking about Dave and wondering if he really had Uncle Hammond's money in the mail sack.

She fidgeted at the dinner table. "Where do you s'pose Dave is now?" she asked.

"He couldn't reach here much before night," Ma observed, "so you and your pa might as well quit watching up the river."

"Dave must be just about heading down Morrison Creek," Pa said, eating fried deer liver as if he were going to a fire.

"You can't hurry him by swallowing your vittles whole," Ma reminded.

Pa gave her a sheepish grin. "Oh, Dave'll make it all right."

Lulie guessed he was thinking the same thing she was: Dave had never had such important mail to carry—$1200 was a terrible lot of money, and the trail from Rock Creek was long and lonesome, with not a homesteader's cabin all the way.

Pa pushed back from the table. "Reckon Log and I had better go find the horses," he said. "Haven't seen hide nor hair of 'em since I got back. Don't want 'em to get to wandering too far away, especially since Ellis Clark claims the Indians ran off with his Blaze."

The horses usually grazed around the hill in the wide meadows toward Elk River. Sometimes they strayed a good many miles. After dinner Pa, Logan, and the dogs struck out to trail them. Spy had got over her limp.

John and Lulie could find nothing to do except hang around the kitchen where Ma was kneading rolls. They watched her sprinkle sugar and cinnamon on the dough.

"Speckle's eggs are a week overdue. I'm sure they're

not going to hatch," Ma said. "Lulie, I wish you and John would go take her off her nest."

Speckle had sat on those eggs so long the feathers on her breast were frazzled and she had shrunk to the size of a robin, but she squawked in protest when Lulie lifted her off.

Tommy, feathers ruffed, came running to see what was happening.

"We're not hurtin' her," explained John. "We're just going to put her out in the sunshine where maybe she'll forget about setting."

Lulie threw away the eggs and filled the nest with sticks. Speckle humped disconsolately in the grass.

"I'm sorry, Speckle," she sympathized. "They were such pretty little eggs!"

John went up the gulch to snare a gopher. Lulie spent some time looking at her autograph album, then got out her brushes and paints and sat down at the table by the front window to try to transfer the glowing purple of lark-spur to paper. If the picture turned out well, she intended to give it to Pa for a present. He was always proud of anything she did. She loved to paint almost as much as she loved to play the organ. For a while she sketched and colored busily.

Glancing out the window, she happened to catch a glint of sun on something bright across the river. An Indian on horseback was coming down the white mineral hill above the cave. The sun had flashed on the rifle he carried. The Crawfords could see Indians traveling that trail almost any time; it was one of their main thoroughfares. The ponies generally picked their way slowly down the hill because it was so steep, but this Indian rode recklessly, and reaching the flat, sent his horse up the valley at a run.

Lulie's eyes narrowed on the horse. It was a long-legged sorrel that stretched out and covered ground like a race horse.

"Why, that's Blaze!" she exclaimed aloud. "I bet anything!"

She ran outside for a better view, but horse and rider were too far away.

Lulie thought Pa and Logan would never get home. When she finally saw them coming, it was almost suppertime. They were leading Kit, who had a little new colt by her side. It was so wobbly they had to travel slowly. She rushed to meet them.

"Kit was hid out," Logan said, "and we had to hunt and hunt for her."

"Thought we'd better find her and the colt before that wolf did," said Pa.

"Pa," Lulie burst out, "I saw an Indian riding Ellis Clark's horse up the valley. He was riding fast, and he had a gun."

Pa frowned. "Could you recognize the Indian?"

"I think it was Piah," said Lulie, "because he kind of stood up in his saddle, and he had a red saddle blanket. Pa, I wish Dave would come."

"I thought sure Dave would beat us in." Pa could not hide his own uneasiness. "It's time he was coming. Maybe I'd better go and see——"

"There he comes right now!" cried Logan. "Yonder—ridin' lickety larrup!"

Usually Coaly reached Steamboat Springs at a weary jog after traveling the long trail from Rock Creek. This time he came at a gallop, with Dave plying a switch at every stride.

"What's got into the boy?" snorted Pa. "He's riding straight into the river! He'll never make it!"

They all sprinted for the riverbank. One minute Coaly was there, fighting to swim; the next, his hoofs were thrashing above the muddy waves, and the horrified watchers could not see Dave anywhere.

Then, a dozen yards down, they glimpsed Dave's checked shirt. Pa leaped along the bank. Fortunately the current whirled Dave into a snag of driftwood where he was able to claw hold of some willows till Pa could reach out and grab him.

Dave lay on the bank, choking and coughing, with Pa trying to pump water out of him. Finally he could gasp, "D-de mail sack——"

"You hurt, Dave?" croaked Pa.

"De s-sack——" Dave jabbered. His face was ash-colored. His teeth clicked with chill from the icy river.

"Easy, boy," said Pa.

Usually Coaly reached Steamboat Springs at a weary jog

"De mail——"

"I see it!" cried Lulie. "Coaly's made it to shore yonder, and the sack's still on the saddle! But oh, Pa," she added in dismay a minute later as she reached the exhausted horse, "the sack's got a big split in it, and the mail's all gone!"

CHAPTER X

The mail was in the river!

It might be carried for miles by the current, or it might be washed ashore almost anywhere. Pa searched the bank frantically, wading the shallow overflow, whacking through the willows and alders. Ellis Clark, who had arrived with the Hayden mail, helped him till darkness finally drove them in.

Pa had sent the children to the cabin long since because he was afraid they might fall into the river. Now he tramped into the kitchen where Ma had Dave wrapped in a blanket by the stove, drinking scalding sage tea. Dave had quit shaking, but his face was woebegone.

"Did you find it?" he cried.

Pa shook his head. He spread a battered newspaper on the table to dry.

Ma tried to be comforting. "I expect the money wasn't even in the sack. It'll probably come in the next mail."

"It was in there," Pa said wearily. "We found the registry receipt. Dave, why'd you try to swim the river?"

"That Injun was a-chasin' me."

"I didn't see any Indian."

"He was layin' fer me up by de hay meadow," Dave declared. "My horse shied, and I seen somepin' shine in de brush like a gun. So I made a run fer it. He chased me and shot at me. I was afeared he'd git me if I waited fer de boat."

Dave broke down and wept. Ponto scrooched as near to him as he could, thrusting a sympathetic nose into his face.

"Never mind, Dave." Pa patted his shoulder. "You thought you were doing the best thing. I'm mighty thankful you weren't drowned."

"But I lost de money!" Dave wailed.

"We'll find it come morning."

After Dave had been bundled off to bed, Pa muttered, "I should never have told him he was carrying money. He's just a boy—with a good imagination. Why would an Indian chase him?"

"To take Uncle Hammond's money," said Lulie.

Pa hooted. "Nobody knew Dave had the money. Anyhow, money doesn't mean much to an Indian. Oh, I don't doubt Dave saw a Ute and that the Ute was running his horse. All the young bucks do. But he wasn't chasing Dave."

Next day there was a sorrel horse limping about the springs across the river.

"Dat's him!" Dave insisted. "Dat's de horse de Injun was a-ridin'."

Pa had no time to look at a horse. He had been up since

daybreak combing the riverbanks for the lost mail. He had not even tasted breakfast.

Ellis Clark got in the boat and went over to see the horse. When he came back, he was angry. "It's Blaze, all right. Some so-and-so's ridden him too hard, and his shoulder's all crippled up again. I put a mud poultice on it."

Lulie nodded. "I knew it was Blaze I saw yesterday afternoon," she said, "and Piah was riding him, I'm almost sure. And I betcha he *was* chasing Dave!"

"Piah," muttered Ellis. "He's one of them renegades always hangin' around Shouse's." He chewed a grass blade thoughtfully. "Could be Blaze goin' lame is what saved Dave. Your Pa's a big man and a fine one. He treats everyone square and expects everyone to treat him square. But I wouldn't trust that Shouse as far as I could throw a bull elk. I reckon you and me had best keep our eyes open."

At first the searchers worked feverishly, knowing paper could not last long in water; and then with slow, heartbreaking thoroughness they probed along the banks.

The morning after the money had been lost, Logan yelled, "I've found it! I've found it!"

Ma and Lulie and John ran to see. Sure enough, yonder was a bit of paper caught on a bobbing willow too far from the bank for them to reach. Afraid every minute it would wash off, they rang the dinner bell to fetch Pa, who was down by the island. He came in great leaping strides and managed to wade out and grab it.

"It's an envelope, all right!" breathed Ma.

"And it has something in it," chattered Lulie, "but it's awfully thin."

The water glued the envelope to whatever was inside, and the whole thing was rotten soft. Ma could not wait for Pa's clumsy thumb to pry it open. She took it and opened it herself. The wet paper tore without a sound. Ma's hands trembled. "It's . . . just a letter," she said, biting her lip in vexation.

Though ordinarily a letter was a wonderful thing to get, they had been so sure they were going to find the money they could hardly stand the disappointment. They could not even read the letter, the ink was so blurred and faded.

Now everybody in the country knew about the money Pa had been expecting, and everybody as far down the river as Hayden was looking for it. Yarmonite's band of Indians helped—men, squaws, and children. Uncle Tow helped, and even Trader Shouse.

"If *he* found it, I bet he'd keep it," Lulie said darkly.

She guessed Trader Shouse would be greedy-glad to get that money, and gladder still to keep Pa from getting it. She felt sure he would be willing to do almost anything to prevent Pa's making his deposit at the land office. Trader Shouse wanted Medicine Springs himself.

Her eyes narrowed in speculation. Could he have bribed Piah—maybe with that shiny gun? The trader could easily have sneaked back to listen at the chinking the night Pa had told the family and Dave about Uncle Hammond's money. His curiosity could have been aroused by Pa's obvious excitement at the supper table. Spy was as afraid of Shouse as she was of Indians, and maybe Shouse had been the reason she could not get to the door and had jumped down the chimney.

"If you could only talk, Spy," Lulie said, smoothing the shepherd dog's silky hair.

As the river went down, Pa kept looking in the cracks in the rocks, poking through drift piles and probing snags where the current might have carried Uncle Hammond's letter with the money in it. He took time out only to bring over the wagon. Ma rejoiced that there was plenty to eat again and that there was coal oil for the lamp.

Gradually the other searchers gave up. Dave and Ellis went back to carrying mail, and the Indians went back to their hunting and horse racing. Uncle Tow drifted off somewhere, and Trader Shouse returned to his camp.

It was Ma who reminded Pa the letter had been registered. "Doesn't that mean the Post Office Department will make good any loss?" she asked.

Pa got out the *Postal Laws and Regulations* that had been sent him with his commission as postmaster and studied it carefully.

"The Post Office Department shall not be liable for the loss of any mail on account of its having been registered," he read aloud, disappointed. "Well, that's plain enough.

Someday maybe that'll be changed, but now registered mail gets special care and that's all."

More than a week had passed since the mail had got lost in the river. Tonight Pa looked bone tired as he tramped up the trail by the Iron Spring.

John and Lulie ran to meet him, crying, "Come see what we found!"

Pa quickened his stride. "You don't mean——"

They tugged him to the shed and there was Speckle with eight greenish balls of fluff around her.

"Wild goslings!" said Pa. "Where did they come from?"

"We found 'em by the river," said Lulie. "They weren't any trouble to pick up. They just stuck their heads in a bunch of grass and thought they were hid!"

"Goslings!" muttered Pa.

"We put 'em in the shed so they wouldn't run away, and Speckle got in through the cat hole and adopted 'em right off!" said John. "Look at her! Isn't she happy!"

The bantam, fluffing her feathers and clucking, was trying to hover her new family. The goslings, almost as big as she was, could not get under her, so they sat around her in a circle and poked their heads under her and made contented sounds.

"Well, Speckle," commented Pa with a wry grin, "you've found a family. I'm glad somebody found something!"

He leaned against the shed door and stared down toward

the river. "We'll spend a few more days looking, and then——"

"Then—Pa?" asked Lulie.

"We'll have to find some way to raise twelve hundred dollars."

CHAPTER XI

Logan poked along the riverbank with his willow fish pole, though for once he was not much interested in fishing. He used the pole mostly to part the grass and bluebells, and prod at tree roots. The water had gone down fast since Dave had nearly drowned, and the envelope containing Uncle Hammond's money might be caught on almost any snag.

But it was not!

Pa had gone several miles below to examine a big pile of driftwood where he thought the envelope might have lodged.

Logan smacked his fishline into the riffles, startling a water ouzel that was hunting periwinkles. The ouzel plummeted to a distant rock and sat there, bobbing nervously.

"If I could walk under water the way you do," Logan grumbled, "maybe I could find what I'm looking for."

His hook floated into the shallows and caught on a grass clump while he swatted at a cloud of mosquitoes. What wouldn't he give to find that money for Pa! Pa hardly ate at all. He hardly slept. He was constantly wet from wading in the river. Ma said he was going to make himself sick.

Trader Shouse, on the other hand, looked fat and happy whenever he rode up to get a drink at the Iron Spring. Too happy. *If he found the money,* Lulie had said, *he'd keep it!*

Suspicion struck Logan. "I betcha he *has* found it, and now it's hid in his tent!" he exclaimed to the water ouzel. "Yessir, I betcha that's it. And I'm goin' to find out!"

He glanced about to see if anyone was watching. John, who had started with him, had put down his fishing pole to transfer his earnest attention to something else—probably mink tracks. Lulie was in the kitchen, learning how to make light bread.

His heart hammering with determination, Logan yanked his hook loose, cached his pole, and waded out to the trail. He fiddled along at first so that if Ma happened to peer through the window, she would think he was just catching grasshoppers, a few of which were beginning to hatch out. Ma would not have let him go. She said Trader Shouse's camp was no place for a boy. Several times last summer Logan had ridden past it with Pa, who would never let him stop. Shucks! Logan could not see why! There were always horse races and other interesting things going on, to judge from the Indians who hung around and the shouts and laughter that he heard. He felt a little guilty sneaking off like this, but Pa and Ma would both be so glad when he found the money!

Spy seemed to be the only one who saw Logan go. She came galloping, with waving tail, to join him.

"Go on home!" he ordered. "Go home!"

He had to throw a stick at her before she would believe he did not want her. Then she cringed, her feelings hurt. He felt bad, too, but he could not have a dog along if he was going to slip into the trader's camp unseen. He'd pet her a lot tonight to make up.

Once beyond sight of the cabin, he ran. The trail humped over small sagebrush hills where Indian paintbrush flowers made splashes of red. After a mile or more it took out across the river bottom, and he could see the smoke from Shouse's camp. He traveled more cautiously, stooping from bush to grass clump and pausing often to peer ahead. A bunch of Indian ponies grazed in the wild pasture. Beyond were other horses with riders on them. The black meadow mold carried the jar and rumble of galloping hoofs, and what he had thought was smoke was dust rising from the race track. He would like to have gone over and watched the excitement, but he had more important business.

At first he could not see Trader Shouse anywhere. There were lots of Indians—more than he had guessed were in the valley. The confusion and festivity made the camp look like a fair. Logan remembered going to a fair once, back in Missouri when he had been a very little boy. Here the bright spots of color were Indian blankets, and he had never heard such kiyi-ing and hollering at the Missouri celebration. He was close enough to tell that most of the Indians were not from Yarmonite's band. He recognized Piah and Colorow, and he'd just as soon not have. Squaws, papooses, and dogs were there, too. He sure hoped those dogs did not get wind of him.

Somebody must have won a race, for the Indians were going wild. Under cover of the din, Logan made it to the edge of the cottonwood grove where the trader's dirty, sagging tent was pitched. Near it lay an old dead tree that Shouse had been using for firewood. The ax was still stuck in the trunk. Logan figured he could crawl along by that tree and reach the tent. He darted forward and flattened on the ground, expecting that any minute one of those pesky dogs would discover him. By and by he risked a peek above the tree stubs and saw the trader's big shoulders hulk through the dust and the crowd. From a pile of stuff on the ground Shouse picked a blanket with a broad yellow stripe and flung it at the Ute who had evidently won the race. The Ute snatched it and rode off, flaunting it, while the kiyi-ing of his friends swelled.

Shouse was not a good loser. He whirled to the horse he had been riding and booted it in the ribs. Logan felt deep disgust.

There was one fortunate thing about it—nobody was looking his way, and he saw his chance to duck under the tent flap. His breath coming fast and hard, he raised up inside the canvas.

Before his eyes had time to accustom themselves to the dusky interior, before he could even take one quick glance around for Uncle Hammond's money, something hurtled from Shouse's bed and set up a torrent of vicious barking, loud enough to wake the dead. As Logan fell back, he realized that one of the Indian dogs must have been stealing a nap on the trader's blankets. Other dogs joined the clamor, and soon the whole camp was in a hullabaloo.

Logan butted out of the tent. Scrambling for safety, he caught his foot on a stake and went sprawling. The next thing he knew, Shouse had him by the collar.

"What you doin' here?" roared the trader.

"N-nuthin'!"

Shouse tightened his grip. "What you sneakin' around fer?"

Logan twisted like a badger. He heard cloth rip, and he was free. Plunging around the woodpile, he stopped, the safety of bristling branches between him and the trader. His neck where Shouse had collared him was hot, and his eyes were hot, too.

"You've got my pa's money," he shouted. "You found it, and you've got it hid!"

"So that's it!" Shouse's roar subsided. He wiped his sleeve across his sweaty face. "No, I ain't got your pa's money. I wish I had. And if this streak of bad luck keeps up, I ain't goin' to have much of anything."

Logan watched him warily, ready to run.

Shouse took out his knife, selected a splinter from the woodpile, and whittled himself a toothpick. "I was shore that hoss would beat them Injun ponies." He kicked at his shadow. "You're gittin' too heavy, Shouse, that's all. If you had somebody light in the saddle——" His eyes fixed on

Logan. He slapped his knee in sudden rough enthusiasm.

"Hey," he said, "that's it! You ride him for me!"

"I—I got to go home," muttered Logan, but he stood watching the trader's stubby fingers ply the toothpick.

"What's your hurry? You can stick on a hoss, cain't you? And I bet you shore would like to make some money to help your pa, wouldn't you?"

"Y-yes . . ."

Shouse's manner became confidential. He explained, "These here Utes have got thirty pony loads of buckskin, and they're keen for hoss racing. I been tryin' to win that buckskin. I've got a good little hoss, but I need somebody light to ride him. You game, son?"

Logan peered at the grass flat, littered with squaws, children, and dogs, and beyond it at the race track where the Indian braves were showing off their ponies.

The trader watched him shrewdly. "I'll whack up with you," he said. "I'll pay you in money for half of whatever we win."

"We-ell," said Logan, his heart thudding with the excitement of what he was about to do, "I might look at the horse."

CHAPTER XII

Logan had always wanted to ride in a race. Though he had galloped Ellis Clark's Blaze up and down the trail by the Iron Spring, that was not the same as racing against another horse. With growing enthusiasm, he followed Trader Shouse across the dusty grass. He knew Pa and Ma did not approve of horse racing, but in this case he thought the end would justify the means. Pa needed money in the worst way, and it would be a fine thing to help him.

The trader had grabbed another blanket from his pile and now waved it in the face of the Utes, his words coming like a torrent. The blindest person would have known he was bragging how he would win this race. The Ute horsemen answered shortly.

Logan began to feel an uneasiness which he tried not to show. The dust was so thick he had not had a good look at Shouse's race horse, and he kept stretching his neck to see it. The Utes paid little attention to him until they found out he was to be the rider; then they crowded around and set up a magpie jabbering.

Shouse put an arm across Logan's shoulders as if the two of them were the best friends in the world, and spewed more words at the Utes. The Utes replied derisively. An

Indian with a yellow moon painted on his forehead had his squaw bring a bundle of buckskin and set it beside Shouse's blanket. He was betting this against the blanket.

Logan looked back once at the trail that led up the valley. He could see Storm Mountain, but he could not see the springs or the log cabin by Soda Creek, and he suddenly felt a long way from home and in a hurry to be through with this business.

"Where's the race horse?" he asked.

"That's him."

Logan stared at the pot-bellied bay with the forelock in his eyes and the scraggly mane. "Why, that's just Podge! That's Uncle Tow's horse!"

"Sure! Fool prospector didn't know he had a race hoss."

The sun was suddenly hot. Logan took off his hat and fanned with it, and Podge gave a snort.

"I loaned old Tow a plug that'll do him just as well," Trader Shouse said. "He's gone up to his claim to grabble out some more nuggets. Thinks he's goin' to buy Podge back."

The trader shortened the stirrups as high as they would go. "Git on, kid, and see how he rides."

Logan climbed aboard. "Get up!" he ordered, nudging Podge with his heels.

The horse flattened its ears and took a nip at him. Yonder Logan could see the long-shanked Indian horses eating up the distance with no effort at all, the Indian riders sitting

cockily on their backs. He could not let them know he had
no faith in his mount. He gave Podge a whack with the end
of the bridle. This time the bay made a half-hearted lunge
and trotted a few steps.

"He won't even run!" cried Logan.

"He will when he gits another hoss alongside him,"
promised Trader Shouse.

The Indians, kiyi-ing like the coyote pups, strutted their
mounts. Logan peered at the horse he had to ride, standing
pigeon-toed and round-bellied, and was thoroughly discour-
aged.

"Look, son," coached the trader, his face red with excitement, "you want to make a good start. It's the first jump
that counts." He broke a willow switch. "This'll help—jest
a lick or two."

Logan's opponent was the half-naked brave with the
yellow moon on his forehead. The Indian continually had
to curb his horse, a nervous, slim-legged dun. Podge stood
with one leg slumped, his ears lopped in boredom; and
Logan sat upon him like a grasshopper. Behind the dun
other horses were waiting—a calico, a buckskin, a slender
blue mare—each bigger and better-looking than Podge.

All Logan wanted now was to get the race over with. The
track was about a quarter-mile down to a crooked willow.
Trader Shouse and most of the Indians stationed themselves there. The din suddenly subsided. The Indian with
the yellow moon ranged his prancing horse alongside
Podge. Logan heard the birds singing in the willows, saw

the cool blue of the sky above the sagebrush. He gripped the switch in one hand and waited.

An Indian with a roach of hair stiffened with vermilion paint down the center of his head was the starter. He brought his arm down swiftly. "Go!"

Logan gave Podge a cut with the switch. Podge jumped like a frog that had almost been stepped on, and landed half a length ahead of the other horse. Off went Logan's hat, but not Logan. He grabbed the saddle horn and hung on. To his surprise, Podge was really running. A gleam of hope came to him.

"Come on! Come on!" he begged.

He heard a thumping that was his heart, all mixed up with pounding hoofs and Indian gibberish and air whipping by.

"Come on!" howled Logan.

The dun was so close that Logan could feel his hot breath. He was bigger than Podge and long-legged, and the crooked willow was too far away. Podge could not win. The Ute was quirting and kicking his pony, and all the other Utes were yelling him on. The track seemed endless. Through the blur of wind in his eyes, Logan could see that the dun was even with him, had passed him. He knew from all the shouting the dun had won the race.

Podge turned around of his own accord and started leisurely for the meadow. Then Logan noticed that the Indians were not celebrating. All the shouting was coming from Trader Shouse.

Off went Logan's hat, but not Logan

He was dancing and yelling, "Hooray! We won!" He reached Logan in a dozen strides and pounded him on the back. "You purty near choked the saddle horn off, but you done it!"

"B-but the Indian was ahead!"

"Not at the crooked willow, he wasn't. You run about twice as fur as need be."

After Podge had rested, he and Logan raced another Indian pony. Logan used the switch just once at the start and left the rest to Podge, and Podge won again. Logan was proud to bursting. He could not understand how little Podge could beat those lean-shanked Indian horses.

"It's like this," explained the trader. "The Utes's hosses is jest as good or better'n Podge, but the riders knocks all the wind out of 'em quirtin' and kickin' 'em. Another thing, them long-built critters don't git started in a quarter-mile. In a half-mile race they'd skin us. Podge, he couldn't keep agoin' that fur."

When Logan slipped into the cabin that night, he was so excited he could hardly eat his supper.

"Where in the world have you been?" asked Ma.

"Down the river," he said—which was the truth, but not all the truth.

Luckily for him, Lulie had had a misfortune with her bread. She had set the sponge on the back of the stove, where it had got too hot and run all over the place. Ma and she were so busy cleaning up the mess they did not take much notice of him. Ma did not even say anything about his torn collar.

Next day, though he had difficulty doing it, he finally eluded Lulie and John, and hurried to the race track. Podge won every race again. The pile of buckskin in front of Trader Shouse's tent grew.

The following day Logan could not manage to sneak away. However, the next afternoon he headed downriver as if he were going to play with Charlie Yarmonite, and then he ran all the way to the race track.

The Indians had sent to another camp for a horse they thought could beat Podge. It was a clean-limbed gray with a slim nose. Piah, the rider, had tied feathers in its tail to help it go as fast as a bird; and he had painted his own eyelids red and his forehead blue. It gave him a most disconcerting appearance.

For the first time Podge came in second best. The Utes went crazy—jumping up and down, yelling, dancing, petting the horse, and thumping Piah. A pile of the buckskin went back to its original owners.

Trader Shouse's hard black eyes screwed up at the corners. He beckoned the Indian riders over to a keg which stood in the shade of his tent. "While the hosses are restin'," he said, "have a drink." He drew some whisky in a cup and passed it to Piah.

Piah liked it so well he demanded more. When the next race was run, the gray horse, with an unsteady Piah atop him, did not win. The bundle of buckskin, along with several horses, went back to Trader Shouse.

The Utes now became sullen. Trader Shouse gave them more whisky out of the barrel. The strong sweet smell of it was in Logan's nostrils. He began to feel sick at his stomach, and he wanted to go home. Besides, the sun was dropping toward Elk Mountain, and the folks would soon be looking for him.

"Please give me my pay," he said.

"Beat it!" growled the trader.

"You said you'd pay me half!"

"If your pa knowed you'd been down here, he'd horse-whip you. But I won't tell him if you beat it now."

Logan blinked hard and doubled his fists. "I won't go till I get my pay!"

Trader Shouse had his hands too full with the Utes to pay much heed to Logan. "Go on! Git!" he ordered the Indians. "No more whisky now. Git, I say!"

Though he shoved and kicked them away from the keg, they came right back, and instead of being pacified, they were beginning to act warlike. One of them flourished a knife. Shouse grabbed a stick and laid about him, and the Indians retreated a short distance.

The sun disappearing behind Elk Mountain seemed a signal for the squaws and children to scuttle back to their camp. The bucks stayed, an angry mutter growing louder among them.

"I want my pay!" bleated Logan, frightened but stubborn.

"You'll git it in a way you ain't lookin' fer, less'n you beat it!" growled Shouse.

At that moment a horseman loomed through the confusion, and Pa's voice demanded, "What's going on here?"

Logan had never been so glad to see anyone in his life. "Pa, he won't pay me!" he cried. "After he promised!"

Trader Shouse shifted uneasily. "The kid come down," he explained, "and I couldn't git him to go home."

"I was tryin' to earn some money to help you," Logan quavered, "and after Podge and me won all those races, he wouldn't pay me!"

Pa, who was on his way home from the drift pile downriver, seemed to discern everything that had happened. He sat in his saddle a minute, his hands across the pommel, his cool, blue gaze looking over the Indians, coming to rest on Shouse with a gleam of abhorrence.

Then he swung off his horse, grabbed the ax from the log, and with one mighty wham knocked the head out of the whisky barrel. The whisky spurted in all directions, making a rank smell in the evening.

The Indians fell back.

"Why, you——" Shouse lunged for Pa.

Pa waited, muscles ready, jaw hard.

The trader paused.

"Shouse," Pa said, and every word was like a punch of his fist, "don't you ever bring whisky into this country again. If you do . . ."

The Indians melted away. All that was left was the dust

on the willows and Trader Shouse standing there, so angry he could only sputter.

Logan climbed up behind Pa's saddle, and they started home. He told Pa the whole story, and he would have felt better if Pa had whaled him good instead of saying in that tired way, "Son, I guess I don't have to warn you that this sort of business is no good."

"No, sir."

After a little, Pa said, "The Utes are stirred up anyhow. This isn't going to help. When they get sober, they'll figure a trick was played on them, and they may do something ugly."

"Do you think they'll come back to Shouse's to get even?"

"Maybe not to Shouse's," Pa said heavily, "but somewhere."

CHAPTER XIII

By the time Logan and Pa reached home after dark, Ma, Lulie, and John had already done the milking and cooked supper. The family took it for granted Logan had been with Pa all afternoon. He wished he had! He wished he had never gone near Shouse's!

Supper did not taste very good to him. His stomach was still in a knot from the stench of whisky and the smell of sweat and dust. He could eat only a spoonful of the Floating Island Pudding Ma had made for dessert.

"Jimmy," Ma reproved, "you mustn't take that boy so far. He's worn out."

"No," Pa said gravely, "I mustn't."

Logan was grateful to him for not mentioning the horse racing or the whisky. He felt pretty foolish ever to have "thrown in" with Trader Shouse.

While the womenfolks put away the supper things, Pa sat by the stove, thawing the chill of river water from his bones. Logan hunched on his stool, suffering from a different kind of chill. He kept seeing Piah and those other Indians who had lost most of their belongings to him and Trader Shouse. When they sobered up, he wondered what they might do.

In the yellow glow of the coal oil lamp, Pa looked tired, but if he was worrying about Indians, he did not let on. He said, "Seems to me I've searched every drift pile and snag from here to Hayden, and I'm afraid we're not going to find Uncle Hammond's money."

"It could have washed clear to the ocean by now," sighed Lulie, "except that paper would come to pieces after being in water so long."

Spy put her nose on Pa's knee, and he petted her absently. "I promised to have the money for the surveyors to take back with them. Reckon I'd better ride to Hahn's Peak and see if Henry and some of the other placer miners can stake me. I might even ask Mr. Farwell."

James V. Farwell, known as the "Merchant Prince of Chicago," was the biggest operator in the Hahn's Peak district.

"Of course the miners'll stake you!" Ma said, brightening.

"Oh, Pa, will you carry a letter to Martha Reid?" cried Lulie.

Martha was the only other white girl in this country near Lulie's age. Her parents ran the boardinghouse at Hahn's Peak, supplying their table with vegetables from their ranch near Elk River. The two girls seldom saw each other, for the Peak was a long twenty-five miles from Steamboat Springs, but they sent letters back and forth whenever anyone could take them.

*

While Pa was at the Peak, Logan stuck close to the cabin and to the big Parker shotgun on the deerhorn rack. He had felt a weight of responsibility since the day before, and eyed every group of visiting Utes anxiously. He was exceedingly relieved when Pa rode home.

"The miners'll be glad to stake us," Pa said, swinging off his horse. "They're going to save up, and when the surveyors are about through with their work, I'll go back to the Peak and get a sack of gold dust. We can repay it a little at a time when we sell our cattle. I didn't even have to ask Mr. Farwell. And," he added, "by the time the surveyors get through, we may have found Uncle Hammond's money."

Pa's cheerfulness was catching. Logan decided Piah and his friends were not going to make any trouble after all. They had probably gone on below somewhere.

And then a peculiar haze crept into the valley.

"Shouse or someone must be burning brush," commented Pa.

By afternoon everyone knew it was not Shouse. A black plume of smoke rose from the pines on Storm Mountain and feathered into the breeze. The family stood in the yard, peering at it.

"How did a fire get started away up there?" asked Ma. "There hasn't been any lightning."

North in the "Bear Country" a second fire sprang up, and that evening when Ellis Clark came in from Hayden with the mail, he reported a third blaze on Sand Mountain.

"Indians!" said Pa grimly.

"Why would they set fire to the trees?" cried Lulie.

"Just gittin' mean," growled Ellis.

Logan knew why. They were mad at him and Shouse. Pa had said they'd get even some way. Beset by a horrible feeling of guilt, he followed Pa to the corral.

"Wisht I'd never raced those horses," he mumbled, digging something hot and stinging out of his eyes.

Pa laid a hand on his shoulder. "Son, I don't reckon you or Shouse had much to do with this."

Together they leaned on the fence, watching the bright stabs of flame in the dusk. After a time Pa said, "One thing is certain—if those fires keep spreading, the whole country'll be ablaze!"

In a few days acres and acres of ancient forests were reduced to black ruin, and smoke rolled out of a dozen new places where the wind had borne sparks. The flames, rapidly eating into the green flanks of the mountains, were fearsome to behold.

Since there was no way for the handful of settlers to put out such a conflagration, they went about their business, measuring the distance from the inferno to their homes with apprehensive eyes. The cabins at Steamboat Springs, deep in the green grass and willows of the valley, seemed in no danger.

However, Pa was worried about the survey. "A township is six miles square," he said. "The line will have to go somewhere along the mountain. I wish the surveyors would come.

And I wish it would rain! Oh, how I wish it would rain!"

Yarmonite's band of Indians, who were now camped across the river half a mile down by the bluff, at first disclaimed any knowledge of the fires. Then one day Charlie Yarmonite rode up on his pony and sat watching Logan split kindling.

"Squaw work," he commented.

"No, boy work," said Lulie, who had come out of the kitchen to empty a pan of dishwater.

Logan stuck his ax in a log and changed the subject. "Charlie, why are the Utes burning the timber?"

For an instant the Indian boy's eyes glittered. "So grass grow for ponies!" he stated—a silly answer because there was already plenty of grass everywhere, and the ponies were fat and fine.

On the Fourth of July the Crawfords could stand in their doorway and watch fireworks to beat any man-made display. Flames, shooting up the pines and spruces on Storm Mountain, looked like giant Roman candles, pinwheels, and skyrockets.

"There won't be any trees left!" moaned Lulie.

The family searched the sky for signs of rain. Day after day the sun blistered down through thickening smoke, and at evening dropped behind Elk Mountain in gory splendor. The moon came up blood red. The wild game fled to the valleys. The children could see deer and elk almost any time; and the smell of bear grew so rank that the horse herd stampeded to Elk River.

"Why can't it rain!" fretted Logan.

While Pa was waiting for the surveyors, he went a short distance up Butcherknife Creek and began to cut wild grass with a hand scythe to make a little haystack. Dave helped him. Dave no longer had to carry mail since the contractor at Hot Sulphur Springs had been able to hire a regular carrier named Mike LeDuc.

"You watch," said Dave. "It's jest natcherly bound to rain now we're tryin' to hay."

He was right. Clouds began to gather, thunderheads boiled over the mountains and burst, and at last the rain poured down.

"This'll put out the fires!" everyone rejoiced.

A few days later smoke was again oozing from Storm Mountain.

"Those fires keep smoldering in the deep dry pine needles the rain can't reach," Pa said. "I'm mightily afraid it will take a winter's snow to put them out."

CHAPTER XIV

Now, nearly every afternoon, lightning ripped the sky, and rain and hail pelted down amid great claps of thunder. Though the showers were violent while they lasted, they were too brief and scattered to do more than slow the forest fires.

During one of these furious thunderstorms, some visitors were swept into Steamboat Springs. When Lulie heard the dogs barking and ran to the door to look, she saw a strange team drawing a hack. The horses had their heads down, fighting the wind, and the mud-spattered hack was swaying under a battering of hail. Two people were huddled on the seat.

"It's a man—and a woman!" she cried.

Ma, apron over her head, ran out. In a jiffy she had bundled the woman into the warm kitchen and was helping unpeel her water-soaked jacket.

"Logan," Ma ordered, "put some more wood in the stove. John, get Ponto out of the way. Lulie, you help me. This is Mrs. Metcalf!"

Ma was as excited as if she were announcing a queen. It had been a long time since she had seen another white woman or heard another white woman's voice!

She went on breathlessly, "You remember, Captain Metcalf came to Steamboat last summer with a hunting party."

"And he liked everything so well he brought me this year," explained the visitor, trying to pry off the hat, which the rain had plastered to her head. She was a little bit of a spunky person with big brown eyes and a sprinkle of freckles across a dainty nose. Right now her teeth were chattering, and her face had an odd pallor. "D-dear me, I didn't know rain could be so wet or so c-cold!"

Ma looked at her sharply. "You're ill," she said.

"Never felt better," insisted Mrs. Metcalf, "except I'm half-frozen and hungry."

"But you're so—*green!*" exclaimed Lulie.

Mrs. Metcalf peered at herself in the mirror over the tin washbasin and began to laugh. "Well, I am a sight! That green veil on my hat must have run in all this rain."

Lulie touched the hat with wonderment. It was fine straw with a wide green ribbon around it and limp webby stuff that must have been yards of veiling. She tried to shape the crown with her fingers. "Maybe if I press it with a hot iron——"

"Never mind about the hat," said the visitor. "It's about gone to seed in all this rain. Mrs. Crawford, I would appreciate it if you could loan me some dry underclothes. I brought a change in the wagon, but I think they're wet, too."

"Of course," Ma said, and hesitated, her face growing pink.

"A chemise and some kind of an old wrapper——" said Mrs. Metcalf.

"I haven't any chemise," Ma had to admit in embarrassment, "except the one I'm wearing."

"Why, Mrs. Crawford!"

The two women looked at each other, and both began to laugh.

"Jimmy didn't bring me any muslin last time he went Outside," Ma said. "He was too busy seeing about a survey. I've patched and patched till there isn't anything left to patch. But never mind. We'll find something dry, though it won't be what you're used to!"

Between them, Ma and Lulie fitted out their guest. She was sitting in front of the oven drying her hair when the Captain came in. He looked thin and tired.

"You march straight into the other room and change your clothes," his wife ordered. "We've found some of Mr. Crawford's you can wear."

"I'm ashamed they're so ragged," Ma apologized.

The Captain had an engaging smile. "Right now I'd rather have them than a king's raiment," he said. "Mrs. Crawford, I never was so glad to get anywhere in my life as to this cabin."

"The Captain has been ill," his wife hastened to explain, "and it was a terrible road in. But he would come. Said if he could just get here and drink that mineral water—well, Captain, don't stand there dripping!"

"No, General," he said, and gave her hair a gentle tweak as he went by.

The rain drove Pa and Dave home. Pa came bursting in and saw the Captain warming by the stove in a pair of his old trousers, hitched on with galluses and turned up at the bottom. "Wondered whose hack that was!" he cried, pumping the Captain's hand. "I'm mighty glad to see you, sir! Mighty glad! And you, ma'am! If I'd known you were coming, I'd have gone to Hot Sulphur to meet you!"

Pa was deeply pleased that Captain Metcalf had thought enough of Steamboat Springs to make the hard trip back with his wife. "We must do everything we can to help him get well and strong again," he told the family.

Next day the Metcalfs moved into the one-room cabin on the hill above Soda Creek, where the Crawfords had first lived. Ma looked at the smoke curling out of the chimney and rejoiced. "Isn't it good to have neighbors!"

"Yes, Maggie, it is," agreed Pa, "and I guess the Metcalfs are not worried over the Indian situation or they wouldn't have come."

Later he asked the Captain, "What's the feeling Outside about the Utes?"

"Oh, the usual. There are always those who say the Indians must go, so settlers won't be afraid for their lives."

"We've lived among the Utes five years and never had any trouble to speak of."

"Wasn't there some shooting in Middle Park last year?" inquired Mrs. Metcalf.

Ma nodded. "The Utes killed Abraham Elliott, a homesteader who'd never done a thing to them. They were just getting even because a white man had shot an Indian named Tabernash near Junction Ranch."

"An eye for an eye and a tooth for a tooth," Pa said. "Did you see any Utes in Middle Park, Captain?"

"As a matter of fact, no. I understand Meeker ordered them all back to the reservation. Seems they'd been killing too many antelope and threatening some of the settlers with 'Big Injun' tactics."

"We saw where they'd been," Mrs. Metcalf added. "They left a trail of fires. All that beautiful timber—such a pity! Why do they do it?"

"I think," Pa said, "to show their dislike for Agent Meeker. He's trying to make plowmen out of roving hunters, and that can't be done overnight."

"Meanwhile, everybody is the loser," commented the Captain. "It will take hundred of years for these forests to grow again."

Mrs. Metcalf bent a quizzical look on Pa. "Mr. Crawford, aren't you ever afraid of the Indians?"

Pa seemed surprised. "It's no use being afraid of anything you have to deal with," he said.

Before the week was out, the Captain had begun to gain weight.

"It's the good thick cream Mrs. Crawford gives us," his wife declared.

"Yes, and the mineral water and pure air," said the Captain, drawing a deep breath. "Mr. Crawford, this is wonderful country. Someday people from all over the United States will come here and call this place blessed."

"That's what I hope!" Pa took off his hat and stood a moment, head thrown back toward the mountains.

The days that followed were happy, in spite of the smoke soiling the deep mountain sky.

At first Mrs. Metcalf sniffed the air a bit uncertainly.

"That's the Big Bubbling Spring you smell," volunteered Logan. "It's got sulphur in it. I like it! Come on and taste it!"

They all started out with a big tin cup. Valiantly the Metcalfs sampled the Big Bubbling Spring, the Heron Spring, the Sweet Spring, the Iron Spring.

"And these are only a few," Pa said proudly. "We've counted a hundred and fifty scattered about—all different temperatures and flavors."

"There's one that'll soft boil eggs," said Lulie. "They never cook too hard."

"And one that looks like milk, but doesn't taste like it," said John, skipping along.

"Come and try the Cold Sulphur Spring!" called Logan.

"Some other time, thank you," sighed Mrs. Metcalf. "I already feel as if I had an apothecary shop inside me!"

There were dozens of other things to show the guests: the beaver house in the pond, the hummingbird's nest on a pine branch, the little lilac bush Ma had transplanted from the old burying ground in Missouri. . . .

Ma could think of no better way to entertain her company than to take them fishing. She loved to fish even better than she loved to cook. She could beat Pa, and she could beat the best fishermen from Hahn's Peak and Hayden. Though the Metcalfs did not complain about the mosquitoes and flies that nearly ate them up and the willows that whacked them in the face, they seemed relieved to get home.

"Mrs. Crawford, I don't see how you do it!" Mrs. Metcalf patted baking soda on a deer fly bite that was swelling above her eye.

Though Ma's face was red and bitten, too, she did not seem to know it. She was holding a trout by its tail and saying triumphantly, "That's the biggest fish I've caught this year!"

Sometimes the women just sat and sewed and talked. Mrs. Metcalf had a way of sounding her words which was not at all like blunt Western speech. Lulie, seated on the elk-hide rug at her feet, drank in the tales of Outside where there were sociables and theaters, and where ladies carried parasoes—just like the picture from *Frank Leslie's Monthly* that she had tacked up on the wall by her bed. Mrs. Metcalf was from Vermont. She had gone to Washington when her father had been a Congressman, and had lived in a gay social whirl. She had even met the President and his lady. Lulie could have listened forever.

The Metcalfs had brought two wonderful things from Outside. The first was a package of oatmeal. Though Ma often cooked corn meal mush, and sometimes made gruel out of coarse graham flour, oatmeal was a delicacy the family had never tried. The other wonderful thing was a bag of lemons. Ordinary lemonade was delicious, but lemonade made with Iron Water was the finest thing any of them had ever tasted. The trick was to mix the juice of half a lemon and a big tablespoon of sugar in the bottom of a cup and stir it while someone poured in the fresh Iron Water. The drink would fizz and run over the top unless a person drank it fast.

Though the lemons were soon gone, Iron Water was pretty good by itself, and there was always plenty of it, bubbling up in the center of the rush-covered mound. It must have been bubbling there for centuries, because all around it the mud was a thick, rusty yellow.

One day Mrs. Metcalf and Lulie were at the spring filling a jug when a dour-looking Indian rode up and got off his pony.

"Me heap catchum," he grunted.

Mrs. Metcalf gathered up her skirts and ran home. Lulie followed with the jug, laughing. "All he meant was he was going to dig some of that yellow paint out of the ground. Didn't you see his digging stick and that buckskin bag?"

"Well, I wasn't sure," Mrs. Metcalf panted, and laughed, too.

It seemed to Lulie the braves these days wore more paint than usual—bright dabs on their cheekbones or down the parts of their hair, and clawed and streaked on their arms and bodies—as if to match the fires on the mountains.

And now, August 1, a fire sprang up in the dry valley grass near Hayden. Ellis Clark brought word of it.

"It burned clear up to the trail by Smart's cabin; the women thought the cabin would burn for sure, and carried out what they could. The cabin didn't catch, but Thompson's hay burned, and Thompson thinks he knows which Indians did it. He's gone to Hot Sulphur Springs to swear out a warrant and get the sheriff to go after 'em."

CHAPTER XV

More than a month later Ellis Clark reported that the sheriff had gone to White River with a posse to try to serve the warrants Thompson had sworn out. But he had been informed by Chief Douglas that no Indian could be arrested by civil process on the reservation, no matter what crimes he might have been guilty of outside that charmed territory. So, rather than stir up more trouble, the sheriff had returned to Hot Sulphur Springs, his trip for nothing; and Thompson had got no satisfaction for his burned hay.

Meanwhile, five whiskered men rode into Steamboat Springs leading pack horses.

Pa took one look and dropped the scythe he was sharpening. "Surveyors!" he boomed, leaping down the trail to meet them. He shook hands warmly and swept his arm in a wide arc. "Welcome to Steamboat Springs, boys!"

The newcomers who, close up, were seen to be young and grinning beneath their whiskers, peered at the sagebrush valley, patched with willows, down which straggled two wagon ruts. They peered at the corral and the handful of log cabins near Soda Creek. They noted the flutter of faded calico as Ma stepped through a doorway, and they saw three wide-eyed children in outgrown clothes, perched on the bank watching them.

Throwing their hats in the air, they shouted, "Hooray for Steamboat Springs!"

Lulie, Logan, and John knew right away they were going to like the surveyors.

Pa invited the men to the cabin for dinner. By the time Ma and Lulie had scurried around to fry several skillets of trout and bake two big panfuls of biscuits, the guests appeared, surprisingly shaven and scrubbed.

"We're quite a bunch to come in on you, Mrs. Crawford," Fred Ingersoll apologized.

"Oh, Ma doesn't mind," said Logan. "She feeds Utes or anybody."

Fred laughed, then clapped a hand to lips swollen with sunburn. "Got to remember to laugh easy," he said, "or they'll crack wide open."

He would have been a nice-looking young man, Lulie thought, if most of the skin had not been blistered off his nose. Ponto took up with him at once and sat on his feet all during dinner.

Fred's crew consisted of a little Englishman named Teddy Milsom and three husky lads he called the "Kansas Boys." The crew wasted little time in talk. They just ate and ate and ate while Ma beamed at them.

"Mrs. Crawford, that's the best meal I ever ate in all my life," Fred declared at last.

"It's the mountain air," Ma said modestly.

After dinner the surveyors pitched camp in the cotton-wood grove across Soda Creek. The ring of axes was exciting.

Lulie, who had a churning to do, turned the crank furiously, first with one hand, then the other, so that she could get through and go watch the men drive tent stakes and stretch canvas. The big square churn stood just outside the milkhouse, in the shade, where she could almost see what was going on, but not quite. At last the butter came, and Ma took it in the wooden bowl to the kitchen to work.

Lulie sped across the footlog and through the willows, and paused to look with favor on the new camp. Fred was tightening tent ropes with an air of quiet competence, and Pa was helping him. One of the Kansas Boys was making a pole table between two trees, while the other two dragged in firewood. Teddy Milsom was stowing away bedding and equipment. John and Logan had a finger in everything.

When camp was in order, Pa and Fred sat down on a log to talk. Fred said, "We'd have been here long ago if it hadn't been for those fires in Middle Park. They put us six weeks behind in our work."

Pa looked over at Storm Mountain. "I hope they don't interfere here. That one is creeping pretty near, but I think we can beat it. Dave and I'll help all we can."

"Good!" said Fred. "Several years ago a man named F. F. Brune ran a line ten or fifteen miles above here, and if we can just find one of his corners it'll save a lot of time. I brought a copy of his field notes."

"What's a corner?" asked Lulie, plumping down on the log by Pa.

"It's a mark or monument placed at the corner of a surveyed tract," explained Fred. "In this case, according to these notes, it's a granite stone sixteen inches by ten inches by eight inches in a mound of stones and marked one notch on the east and five on the west."

"I believe we can find it!" said Pa.

And find it they did after a day's search. Pa was triumphant. "It's on Yellow Jacket Pass, right in the thick brush. We never would have located it if it hadn't been for those field notes."

"And if you hadn't known the country so well," said Fred. "Tomorrow we can begin the survey."

There was something momentous in the very word. The survey was what Pa had been waiting for all summer. It was a necessary step to ownership of the land.

Since it was now September and the days were shortening toward winter, the men had to make every moment count. They rode off at dawn and returned at dusk. As Pa saddled and unsaddled, the strains of "Flow Gently, Sweet Afton" floated back from the corral. The work was going well.

The children wanted to watch the survey.

"Sure," said Fred, "you can help us run a line."

And so, in great excitement one morning they set forth, Lulie riding Puss with John behind her, and Logan riding Monty. They splashed across the river, which was now low enough to be forded easily, and proceeded over the hill and up the valley. Spy trotted sedately behind, and Ponto lumbered everywhere.

Smoke from the forest fires had settled like fog, thinned here and there by the breeze. Suddenly the riders found themselves in the midst of a herd of elk that were drifting out of the spruce timber to drink at the river. The elk were not greatly disturbed. A few of them, pestered by Ponto, tore by on a gangling run, but the rest continued to the river.

Half a mile farther on, a grizzly bear reared up in the trail. Even Ponto knew better than to tease a grizzly. The horses did not wait to see the bear's great frosty head and the slobbers running out of his mouth. They twisted themselves wrong side out to get away. Puss plunged and bucked, Lulie and John clinging to her like burs. The other horses scattered over the country but were finally urged back to the trail again, snorting and trembling.

"After all, the bear was here first," Pa said. "I reckon it's his country."

"Well," commented Fred, "we're putting the white man's mark on it now. He'll have to move back to the mountains."

The men found the spot where they had quit yesterday, and dismounted with their equipment. Dave would take care of the horses, herding them along till the men needed them again for riding home. Lulie and Logan took care of their own horses, sometimes riding, sometimes walking and leading them.

A grizzly reared up in the trail

Fred lifted his compass from its leather case and affixed it to the tripod. He leveled it and squinted through the peep sights.

"What are you doing?" asked John.

"I'm seeing that we go the proper direction," said Fred. "Yesterday before we quit I set my compass by the sun, so now we can start right out."

"I thought a compass needle always pointed north," ventured Lulie.

"Not in a country where there are so many minerals as here. The needle is often pulled off true. The only way I can be certain we are headed right is to take a reading by the sun, and I can do that with this attachment."

"Let me look!" cried Logan.

"See," said Fred, "the sun's rays pass through a little opening onto this silver reflector where a small image of the sun is formed in the center of two fine lines. Here is an arc that I can read and from it determine the true meridian. Then all I have to do is turn my sights to it and take my course. Well, here we go! The chainmen do the actual measuring by carrying this chain—one on each end."

"You bet," boasted Teddy Milsom. "We do the important work!"

He grabbed a brass handle and went crashing through the brush, dragging the chain, which was composed of a hundred links of heavy steel wire. He moved to right or left as Fred indicated by a wave of his arm. One of the Kansas Boys held the other end at the last station point until the chain was stretched taut. At that place the leader drove a steel pin in the ground. It had a red rag tied to it so that it could easily be seen. The follower picked up the first end and carried it with him to the station just established, and the process was repeated. The follower gathered up the pins as he came to them. When he had collected ten, he handed them over to the leader, and they went through the same procedure again. Fred said it took eighty chains to make a mile.

Where there were trees in the way or too much brush, the axman had to chop them out. "I do the heavy work," he grumbled good-naturedly.

Every half-mile the moundsman set a permanent marker. He hunted up a stone of proper size and placed it solidly in a mound of stones, after first notching it with a few gouges of his chisel. Every notch meant something. Where there was no stone handy, he drove a marked post into the ground, charring it first so that it would not rot in the earth. Then the axman blazed a nearby tree on the side facing the corner.

"Why are you doing that?" Logan wanted to know.

"So it'll be easier to find the corner if anybody's looking for it," said the axman. "This is called a bearing or witness tree."

Fred kept careful notes on everything that was done, and Pa lent a hand wherever it was needed.

They ate their lunch by a small creek. John took advantage of the opportunity to climb on a rock and peer through the peep sights of the compass, which Fred Ingersoll had carefully set down. Squinting his eyes like Fred, he announced, "I see four bear!"

"Great Scott!" Fred jerked to attention. "Where?"

"He doesn't mean four," Lulie explained patiently. "He just says four because he likes the sound of it. And he's always seeing bear even when there aren't any."

Fred laughed. "Well then, come on, Four-Bear-Boy! We'd better get going. We've a long way to travel."

The surveyors marched through willows and sagebrush, and across game trails worn one foot deep into the grass roots.

"Someday there'll be ranches all over this valley," prophesied Pa.

Lulie could almost see them now—houses, fences, haystacks. She felt a small pang that the beautiful unspoiled land would have to fit itself to the measurements the surveyors made. It would never again be free and wild. It would never again belong to the bear and the elk. Fred said it would be labeled on a map *Township 6 North, Range 84 West*, and this label would link it forever with the rest of the civilized United States.

Late that afternoon, as they rode home, Pa and Logan stopped to kill a deer while the rest continued on.

Several Indians on horseback were waiting at the surveyors' camp.

"Oh, oh! Who's our company?" murmured Fred.

At first Lulie thought they were some of Yarmonite's

band who had come to the camp a time or two, apparently out of friendly curiosity. She soon saw they were not.

"One of 'em's Piah," she said, trying not to look startled, "and one is Colorow."

Spy dived into the nearest tent.

"Hello!" said Fred.

The visitors merely stared. The sun was gone, but its fire seemed to linger in the vermilion and ocher of weirdly painted faces.

With a shrug, Fred dismounted, as did the other men. They untied their equipment and unsaddled their horses. Teddy Milsom began to gather sticks to build a fire. Lulie, held by an intense feeling that something was about to happen, sat there on Puss, wishing Pa and Logan had not stopped to kill that deer. She felt John's arms tighten around her.

"What you do here?" Piah demanded of the surveyors.

"We're working for Mr. Crawford," Fred told him.

With a haughty manner Piah indicated the compass in its leather case. "You drive sticks in ground and chop trees. Make marks. Many white men come. Build fence. Take Ute country."

"Hey now, wait a minute!" cried Fred.

Piah gestured violently. "Utes have to go away. No more grass for ponies. No more ponies. No more hunt."

The Indians all had guns. The surveyors were unarmed except for Teddy, who had a rifle leaning against a tree. He was about to reach for it when Fred snapped, "Hold it!"

Not a breath of air stirred in the grove. Not a leaf moved.

Piah slid from his pony. With his long finger he scratched in the ground. "Utes' dirt!" he grunted. "One sleep, you go!"

CHAPTER XVI

In spite of Piah's threat, the surveyors kept doggedly at their work, though some days they were only a short distance from the blazing forests, and returned to camp at night with smoke-reddened eyes.

"We never quit a job halfway," Fred said tersely, "and we don't intend to quit this one just because some Ute is trying to be 'Big Injun.' "

"When I first came to this valley," Pa recollected, "the Utes told me 'One moon, you go,' and I'm still here."

The newspaper, printed in Denver and packed across two mountain ranges on horseback, carried headlines about the fires that were raging all over northwestern Colorado, but settlers along Bear River had been looking at smoke and fires all summer and were getting used to them. If the children had to go after the cows late, they watched the red glow on the range curiously, and noted the small, twinkling fires of Yarmonite's tepee village in the other direction.

When Pa came home from helping with the survey, his clothes smelled of smoke, and Ma could not keep them mended. They were threadbare anyhow from a winter's wear and from chopping and hauling building logs for a barn.

Ma cut off the trouser legs at the knee and turned them hind side before so that the worn part would be underneath. Next night Pa's knees were out again!

Pa took to wearing his elk-hide trousers. They were all right till they got wet and stretched when he waded the creek; then they dried with a permanent bend at the knee.

"For heaven's sake, man," joked Fred, "if you're going to jump, jump!"

Pa grinned, but Ma did not like to have him going around looking like a tramp—especially now that the survey was almost finished and it was time for him to ride to Hahn's Peak to get the gold dust the miners had promised him. Though she dampened and pulled and pressed those elk-hide trousers, trying to coax them back to shape, they stayed baggy.

"They'll do, Maggie," said Pa. "They'll have to."

Lulie wrote another letter to Martha Reid. "Pa, I invited her down to visit," she said. "Maybe she can come back with you."

Pa had no sooner ridden off on Monty than Ma dug out a piece of canvas from the storeroom, and spread it on the floor, looking at it critically.

"Whatcha goin' to do with our old wagon sheet, Ma?" asked John.

"I'm going to make your pa a new pair of pants!" declared Ma.

The canvas, which had been used to spread over a wagon

to protect its contents from rain and dust, was a weather-streaked gray, and there was a big spot of grease on it. By the time Ma and Lulie had scrubbed it, bleached and dried it in the grass and pressed it, it looked almost white. They ripped up a pair of Pa's old pants to get a pattern; then they began to sew, using the three-cornered needles that Ma generally used for sewing buckskin.

Mrs. Metcalf came down to help, but since only two could work on the trousers at a time, she offered to cook dinner. Ma and Lulie heard her shake down the ashes in the stove, heard her go out to chop some kindling.

It was just as well they could not see her. The Vermont Congressman's daughter was not used to chopping wood. Even here in the wilds the Captain always kept her supplied, but today he had gone with the surveyors. Logan, who had forgotten to fill the woodbox, was in the meadow with John, helping Dave spread the hay to dry.

Ponto was the only one around, and he came wagging up just as Mrs. Metcalf whammed the ax blade down. With a yelp, Ponto jumped away, leaving the proud yellow tassle from the tip of his tail on the chopping block.

He skulked off, ashamed of his tail, and Mrs. Metcalf took a fresh grip on the ax. "I'm sorry, dog," she muttered.

Later Lulie remarked, "Wonder what happened to Ponto's tail?"

Mrs. Metcalf was very busy, and Ponto could not talk.

He stayed in the dark corner under the table the rest of the day.

Ma and Lulie were sewing as hard as they could, and Mrs. Metcalf was washing dishes when they heard—of all things—a bugle! They dropped what they were doing and rushed to the door. There, drawn up in the flat near the Iron Spring, was a troop of cavalrymen. Logan, John, and Dave left their willow pitchforks and came running, all eyes for the blue uniforms and bright buttons and soldier caps. The faces that looked out from under those caps were as dusky as Dave's, for this was a Negro troop except for the captain, the lieutenant, and the guide.

Lulie recognized the guide as Sandy Mellen, a friend the Crawfords had known in Middle Park. He was jaunty and young, but already stamped with the ruggedness of the frontier and more at home in his saddle than even the cavalrymen. Now he was grinning at the two little red-headed boys and young Negro lad, who stared, breathless, at the dusty glory of real, honest-to-goodness soldiers.

It was at his suggestion, no doubt, that the bugle sounded again, and the troop snapped through maneuvers. They formed a line, about-faced, wheeled right or left at the command. They presented sabers, charged sabers, and returned sabers. Then they dismounted, and the two officers strode up the trail, their bright spurs jingling.

Cap in hand, the captain presented his compliments to Ma. "Captain Dodge, ma'am—ninth U.S. Cavalry—at your service! And this is Lieutenant Hughes. We've been Below and are on our way back to Middle Park."

"You've been Below?" Ma asked quickly. "Did you find trouble?"

"Nothing much." The captain shrugged. "A few Utes stealing food and annuities."

"Do you think there's real danger from the Indians?"

"No, ma'am. If I did, I wouldn't be returning to Middle Park."

Sandy Mellen strolled up. "The captain was going on through Twenty Mile Park and miss Steamboat Springs till I told him this was a better way to come." Sandy winked at Logan and said behind his hand, "I wanted a drink of Iron Water and a good bath, and it's only a few miles farther."

"Come in and rest a while," invited Ma.

She heaped a plate with sugar cookies and sent Lulie to the milkhouse for a pitcher of buttermilk. "I wish I had enough for all those tired troopers," she said.

Captain Dodge and the lieutenant leaned back in their chairs. It had been a long time since they had sat in chairs and longer still since they had tasted buttermilk. While Ma and Mrs. Metcalf conversed with them about the Indians and the forest fires, the children captured Sandy. He was never much of a talker, but when they could get him started he was better than a story book. Today, with a fistful of cookies, he was willing to prolong his visit as long as possible. He had been more places and done more things than anybody they knew. He had split ties for the Union Pacific in Wyoming, hunted for the market, prospected at Hahn's Peak, carried mail, even cooked for the construction gang building Berthoud Pass road.

The troopers, too, were making the most of their stay. They drank at the Iron Spring and sprawled on the ground, and some of them slept in the shade of the cottonwoods. Their horses, dragging bridles, nipped the salt grass.

When Sandy insisted he had run out of tales, Logan and John went to see the troopers and admire their swords. One big fellow asked Logan, "Got any tobaccy, son?"

Logan hesitated. He knew where Pa had a little hidden away, which he smoked sparingly, but it would nowhere go around among forty-four troopers, so he shook his head.

When the supply wagons had caught up and the teams and drivers had had a chance to rest, Captain Dodge gave the order for the men to mount.

"We'll take our time going back to Middle Park," he told Ma. "I think we'll stop at the Bath Spring and then go on to Egeria Creek and camp a while."

The column rode leisurely up the valley. Sandy, at the head with the captain, turned to wave before the willows hid him.

"I feel relieved," Ma exclaimed. "If there was any real danger from the Indians, Captain Dodge would surely know it."

Moving into the spot of sunshine from the window, she continued her sewing. Lulie had finished all she could do on the trousers and was seated on the floor with Dick Woodchuck a furry ball in her lap. His cousins had already hibernated, although it seemed early. Not one was to be seen around the Bent Cottonwood or the rocks of the ridge. All Dick did was eat and sleep.

Mrs. Metcalf, who was reading aloud from the *Youth's Companion,* broke off in the middle of a sentence with a surprised "Oh!"

Yarmonite stood in the doorway. "What soldiers do here?" The sharpness of the September wind edged his words.

"Just riding through," Ma told him.

Yarmonite's eyes, one clouded, one smoke-reddened, seemed to be staring at something beyond this comfortable cabin room.

"Soldiers make trouble!"

"No, Yarmonite." Ma tried to reassure him. "Soldiers not make trouble. Just going to camp in Middle Park." She knotted her thread. "Lulie, you go fix Yarmonite some bread and molasses."

Dumping Dick Woodchuck from her lap, Lulie went to the kitchen. She cut a big slice of bread, buttered it generously, and spread it with the thick golden syrup which the Indians liked so much.

When she looked for Yarmonite, expecting to find him

squatted outside the door, he was not there. Yonder he stood, peering into the Big Bubbling Spring as he had that day last spring when Tabby had been so sick. Without turning to glance back, he got on his pony and rode down the trail.

"I wonder why he didn't wait!" cried Lulie.

CHAPTER XVII

Next day near noon, when Pa returned from the Peak, Ma took him into the back room first thing and showed him the neatly pressed white trousers on the bed.

"Well, I'll be switched!" he cried, holding them up to him. "A brand-new pair of pants. And as fine ones as I've ever laid eyes on! Maggie, where . . . ?"

"The wagon sheet!"

"That dirty old canvas? Maggie, you're joking. Some expert tailor came along and you bought them."

"Lulie and I sewed on them all day yesterday," Ma said. "I broke my best needle."

Pa caught her in his arms and kissed her. "I've never had a pair of pants that suited me so well! Nosireebobtail Peter horsefly!"

"Now," beamed Ma, "you can go to the land office looking halfway decent."

"Yes—the land office." The letdown way Pa said that made Ma look at him sharply.

"Jimmy, you didn't get the gold dust."

"No, I didn't. There's no placering being done at the Peak."

"No placering!"

"Nearly everybody's left the Peak. There are only nine men in camp, and they haven't had time to do any placering for trying to keep the forest fire from burning the buildings and the wooden flumes."

"But Mr. Farwell——" began Ma.

"Farwell's sold his holdings to somebody in Rawlins. Couldn't make operations pay."

"Why didn't Henry and Nannie let us know?" cried Ma.

"They did. Sent a letter by Trader Shouse a month ago. Shouse was up there doing some swapping."

"And he never delivered it!" exclaimed Lulie.

"No." Pa's jaw was hard. "I came by his camp and he's gone. Probably halfway to Denver by now with his summer's loot, and, from all signs, driving quite a herd of horses."

Ma's eyes snapped. "Jimmy, if that rascal could get to the land office and had the money, could he——"

"I don't know. The land office agreed to protect our rights until the surveyors returned, but they were stretching a point to do that. The deposit is usually required before the survey begins. If we can't send the money by the surveyors, and Shouse shows up with cash enough——"

Pa stared out the window. "I could raise a little by selling our cows if I had time to drive them to market."

The sour milk Ma had set in a pan on the back of the stove was getting too hot to make good cheese, but Ma did not seem to notice. She said, "Jimmy, we can't spare our cows. Maybe Captain Metcalf will help us."

"That he will!" declared a hearty voice from the doorway. The Captain had come down the trail in time to overhear Ma's last remark. He was no longer the thin, tired man who had driven into Steamboat Springs some weeks ago. He walked with a spring in his step, and there was meat on his bones. Mrs. Metcalf and he were getting ready to go back to Denver before snow came on the range. "If it's an errand I can do for you Outside, or anything else, just name it."

Pa fidgeted. It went against his pride to admit financial embarrassment to the Captain.

Ma said right out, "We need twelve hundred dollars to pay for this survey, and it's nothing to be ashamed of." She told how the money had been lost in the river and how the miners at Hahn's Peak had promised to stake Pa, and how circumstances had prevented them. And she told how the surveyors were leaving tomorrow, and Pa did not know a soul in Denver who might help him.

"Well, I do!" The Captain pounded the table till Tommy Bantam, who had been searching for crumbs under it, gave a startled croak. "I'm well acquainted with my bankers. They make loans every day to less deserving people. There'll be no trouble——"

It was all fixed—as easy as that! Ever since June the money had been a load on their minds, and now in less time than it had taken the milk to boil over on the stove, the load was lifted.

"We were going to leave in a day or two anyway," said

the Captain. "We'll get ready right away and go out tomorrow with you and the surveyors."

Pa wrung the Captain's hand and hurried off to grease the wagon, for he would take it to bring back a load of supplies.

Captain Metcalf strode up the trail to help Mrs. Metcalf pack.

"Oh dear," moaned Lulie, "I wish everyone wasn't going away!"

Ma sprinkled a pinch of sugar on the stove so that the burned milk would not smell so bad. "I guess we'll just have to——"

"I know—make the best of it!" Lulie burst out. "I'm tired of doing that!"

The minute she had said it she was sorry. All at once she could see how lonesome Ma looked, standing there in the empty kitchen and peering out the window where there was nothing to see except hills and more hills.

Tommy Bantam flew up on the table to snatch a big beakful of cheese. Lulie caught him and put him on her shoulder.

"Anyhow, we have Tommy," she said resolutely. "He's pretty good company."

The cabin was not empty long. When the mail carrier hallooed up the valley and then splashed his horse across Soda Creek and swung the mail sack from the saddle, everybody in Steamboat Springs rushed to see what he had brought.

Pa unlocked the mail pouch. The first thing he took out was the *Rocky Mountain News*. Spreading it on the table, he read aloud: "Agent Meeker warns he can no longer control Utes. Settlers on Bear and Snake Rivers must look out for themselves."

They all crowded around to try to read over Pa's shoulder or under his arm. There were a few letters, but no one picked them up.

"Jimmy," Ma whispered, "what does it mean?"

"Oh, the newspaper's always hollering about the Indians," Pa growled. "I'll go see Yarmonite and find out."

He threw a saddle on Monty and rode down to the Ute camp. In a short time he returned to report that the Indian camp was deserted, and the trail down country littered with broken tepee poles. "They must have left in a hurry," he frowned. "I don't know what to think."

"We've always looked out for ourselves anyway," Ma said sturdily, "and if the Indians have gone on down country, there's nothing to worry about."

"I wish I knew," muttered Pa. "Denver's a long way off."

"You've got to go and protect your land rights," stated Captain Metcalf. "Why not let me stay here to look after things till you return? I'll write a letter you can take to the bank. It'll do as well as if I went."

"If there's danger," said Pa, "I couldn't let you stay. You must get your wife home."

"I'm not going!" Mrs. Metcalf squeezed Ma's hand. "I

wasn't ready anyway. I want to pick some more choke-cherries."

"Then it's settled!" declared the Captain. "I'll go write that letter."

*

Now it was almost dark. Frank and Peggy were picketed nearby, where they could be quickly brought in and har-nessed in the morning. The supplies for the journey were packed.

In the red smudge of evening the family sat on the shelv-ing rocks back of the cabin while Pa and Ma talked. Though the September air was sharp, the rocks were still warm from the sun. A small garter snake rippled through the dry leaves, but not even John had heart enough to chase it. Logan sat popping the dry seeds from a clump of bladderpod.

Lulie hunched at Pa's knee, knowing that tomorrow he would be a long way off. She thought of the deserted Indian camp. Why had Yarmonite's band gone away so suddenly and without a word? She thought of the notice in the newspaper.

Ma said, "Jimmy, if the Indians come, what shall I do?"

Selecting a stick of sagebrush, Pa took out his pocket-knife and began to whittle. Down in the corral the cowbell tinkled, and somewhere on Copper Ridge a fox barked. Blackbirds, flying to roost, made a dry chatter.

"Well, Maggie," Pa said at last, "I don't believe the Indians will come, but if they do, you and the children had better go up Soda Creek. There are a few white people in North Park, and you must try to work your way over to them."

Lulie stared up Soda Creek where black, mysterious mountains rose above the familiar hills. She shivered.

CHAPTER XVIII

What an empty place Steamboat Springs was with Pa and the surveyors gone! Lulie was wondering how she could ever stand the lonesomeness when a wagon rattled in from Elk River. It stopped in front of the cabin, spilling out four children, a sunbonneted woman, and a man with red chin whiskers.

"It's the Reids!" she shrieked, running to throw her arms around Martha. "You got my letter. You did come!"

"Yes, but we were coming anyway," said Martha, giving a skip that made her flaxen braids jump. "We're moving."

"To Hayden," chimed in small Vada, clutching a striped kitten that was hissing at Ponto.

"But we're going to camp here ever so long," volunteered Addie, "and bathe, because Mama said there'd be enough hot water for once."

"That's just what I told Samuel." Mrs. Reid laughed, taking off her bonnet and fanning herself with it. "I intend to take a bath every single day in that good hot spring."

"I'm so glad—so glad you came!" cried Ma.

"You womenfolks'll have plenty of time to visit." Mr. Reid's chin whiskers bobbed up and down as he talked. "Albert and I will go on down to the hay ranch at Hayden and build us a cabin."

"No use staying around the Peak any more," said Albert, a tall, thin, nearly grown boy. "Everybody and the dog's moving away."

The Reids made camp across Soda Creek. While Albert and Mr. Reid were driving tent stakes and Mrs. Reid was airing bedding on the grass, Lulie linked her arm in Martha's and suggested, "Come on, let's go over to the storehouse."

John and Logan had already escorted the little girls there and were stuffing their pockets with sweet, sugary raisins that came packed in layers in a wooden box. Martha and Lulie dipped into the box, too; then they all went to the Iron Spring for a drink of water and back to camp, where Mr. Metcalf was asking Mr. Reid what he knew about the Indians.

Mr. Reid was chopping up a dead alder for firewood. He leaned on his ax. "This is the first year I've ever wished for winter," he said. "The Utes always leave the snow country. I hope they've already started for the reservation, and I hope the storms come soon to put out those dratted fires!"

Next morning he and Albert hitched the team to the wagon and went to Hayden, while the rest of the family settled down to having a good time. Ma and Mrs. Reid made up for the long, lonesome months when they had had no other woman to visit with; and Mrs. Metcalf, small and lovely, from a magical place called "the East," was their darling.

"I'm so glad I came!" Mrs. Reid said over and over.

The children played endless games of croquet, "catch," and hide-and-seek. They followed the leader, hopping from mound to mound among the springs and laughing and squealing. Logan and John led excursions into the willows, but not too far, for the willows were wilderness where there were always bear tracks, "smoking fresh."

Vada and Addie were more interested in giving tea parties for their rag dolls, with acorn cups arranged on a rock and all kinds of "choclit" pies and cakes patted out of the sticky red clay. The rag dolls were not pretty like Annie. Most of the paint had been kissed from their flat round faces, and they had no shoes at all. The little girls were fascinated by Annie's beautiful blue kid shoes, dainty kid fingers, and perfectly curled black porcelain hair.

Annie's miniature footgear reminded Lulie of the real blue shoes in Trader Shouse's pack which she had once tried on. With a pang she wondered what Yarmonite's squaw had done with them. If Vada and Addie could see those, wouldn't their eyes pop!

Annie was always guest of honor and sat on her quilt with quiet dignity, because, Lulie explained, "Annie's a grown-up doll. She doesn't like to play in the dirt."

However, Annie was not too grown up to attend school when Martha and Lulie took turns being teacher. School was held near the Bent Cottonwood so that Lulie could play the organ for opening exercises. Vada, Addie, and the rag dolls came, and so did John, when he was not too busy looking at his mink traps. But Spy hid out, and Fleet and Fanny ran off to the woods somewhere, and Ponto would not sit down and behave. Not even Dick Woodchuck was there. He had disappeared, and Ma said no doubt he had found a good hole and gone to bed.

"Come on, Logan," wheedled Lulie, "we need more scholars. Be a good boy and come to school!"

Logan was feeling important these days, for he had had a birthday on the nineteenth and was ten years old. Ma had baked him a special cake with beaten cream icing.

"If it's singing school, maybe I will," said Logan, looking cross-eyed at his nose. He caroled:

> "Oh, the singing school is beautifool,
> Oh, the singing school is beautifool!
> If I had you for my teacher,
> I would be a happy creature,
> For I dote upon the singing school!"

Fishing was more to his liking. Nearly every day the children caught grasshoppers and threw in their hooks at the mouth of Soda Creek or by the Big Rock in the river.

Ma would have fished, too, if her guests had not preferred to sit and visit. When the children caught more fish than could be eaten at once, she packed them in brine for use later. She "put down" butter in jars against the time when the cows would have to be driven to winter range in Burns's Hole. Every evening she would say, "Well, I guess your

Pa's camped at Finger Rock.'" Or, "I guess he's on Gore
Range." Or, "He must be coming down into Middle Park.
I'll be so relieved when he gets home!"

Meanwhile, in Bear River valley, nights were frosty, but
days were warm and sunny. The chokecherries on the
bushes back of the cabin were dead ripe. The children's
mouths were stained from eating them. Speckle's geese
stretched their wings, unlimbered their necks, and listened
to the wild jabber in the rushes, while Speckle sang and
gave more attention to Tommy.

Lulie and Martha spent hours looking at their autograph
albums. Such small, precious booklets! Martha's had a
yellow plush cover adorned with an ivory fan, and Lulie's
bore a picture of a pink rose twined with lilies of the valley.

"Almost all the miners at Hahn's Peak wrote in mine,"
said Martha.

"Mine, too," said Lulie. "When they get rheumatism
working in the sluices, they always come down here to soak
in the hot spring. But I guess they won't any more," she
added, "if they're all moving away."

"Oh, Papa says they'll be back next spring. He says there's
lots of gold at Hahn's Peak yet. I like what Frank Wood
wrote the best. Listen.

> 'In memory's casket
> Drop one pearl for me.'

Isn't that simply beautiful! And see how he shaded his
letters!"

"Why, that's the very same thing he wrote in mine!" exclaimed Lulie.

Heads together, they pored over each page. Lulie had examined her album so many times she knew everything in it by heart, from the honest simplicity of

> "Remember well, and bear in mind
>   A trusty friend is hard to find,"

signed by Ellis Clark, to the exquisite sadness of:

> "Passing years may throw
>   Shadows on thy brow so fair,
> Steal from thy rich cheek its glow
>   Silver thy dark hair.
> Live a woman firm and true,
>   Changeless with each passing breath;
> Nerve thy soul by noble deeds
>   To cope at last with death."

Aunt Nannie had copied this from a magazine. Some of the contributors had inscribed their own inspirations, illustrated with pencil or ink sketches or even oil paintings. All had done their painstaking best.

Pa had written only his name in clear sturdy letters, and on the opposite page Ma had written hers and the date in old-fashioned curlicues, with a fine pen and great care. Even Logan had written: "Dear Sister: In this book you will see your brother's name." Only he had made a mistake

Heads together, they pored over each page

and written *mane*, and signed his name with a flourish which he hoped was like Pa's.

"I have a good one to write in your album," said Martha, "and I brought some purple ink. Mama was afraid it would spill all over everything."

They went down to the Bent Cottonwood for privacy, and seated themselves by the organ, which now became a table to write on. Since the woodchucks had gone to bed for the winter, there was nothing to disturb them except a green-tailed towhee that flirted through the underbrush, asking the same husky question over and over.

Opening Lulie's album to a fresh page, Martha lavishly embellished it with "boughten" stickers that someone had brought her from Rawlins. At the top she pasted two white doves ringed with forget-me-nots; in the center a peacock with a trailing purple tail; and at the bottom an amazing blue, green, and red bird on a nest made of roses. Around these decorations she slowly wrote:

> "Friendship is a golden chain
>   That binds our hearts together;
> And if we never break that chain,
>   We will be friends forever.
>   Your truly friend and sister,
>   Martha Reid"

In Martha's album Lulie copied four lines from a poetry book a Missouri cousin had sent her:

"Full many a gem of purest ray serene
The dark unfathom'd caves of ocean bear;
Full many a flower is born to blush unseen,
And waste its sweetness on the desert air."

Lacking stickers to paste in her friend's book, she painted a bunch of rose apples and autumn leaves, matching her colors with the vivid display all about her.

*

It was now September 29, and Pa had been gone four days. Ma had just lifted a serviceberry pie from the oven when Speckle's geese, sunning in the trail, broke the noon stillness with disturbed gabbling.

Logan, sloshing a bucket of water up from the creek, cried, "Here comes someone!"

They all ran out to see who it was. A horse tottered to the cabin, and a white man—a stranger—almost fell from the saddle. His face was gray with weariness. His bloodshot eyes searched anxiously.

"Cap'n Dodge!" he croaked.

Ma, a pot lifter still in her hand, said quickly, "He's not here. He was through here several days ago, but he went on to Egeria Creek."

The man slumped with disappointment. He caught the horse's mane to steady himself. "Got to git him!" his cracked lips whispered.

"What's happened?" cried Ma. "Who are you?"

"Meeker sent me . . . trouble . . . even now . . ."

"Come in! Come in and sit down."

"No, got to go on," muttered the man.

But Ma had firm hold of him, and by then Captain Metcalf had come, and between them they got him into the cabin and spooned some hot soup down him.

"Ain't eat nuthin' since yesterday morning," mumbled the man.

"Dave, take care of that tired horse," Ma said. "Feed him some of the corn chop we have for the chickens and rub him down."

"Pore critter's been rode so hard he's got the thumps," said Dave.

A little rest and food revived the man, who told them that his name was Ed Mansfield and he worked at the Indian Agency. He said the Utes had started a war dance and had fired upon the white employees who were trying to plow, and that Agent Meeker and his wife and daughter did not dare come out of their house.

"The War Department's sending troops from Fort Steele, Wyoming," the messenger went on hurriedly. "One hundred and ninety men and twenty-five supply wagons, but Meeker's afraid they won't get there in time. No telling what's happened by now," he croaked, pulling to his feet. "I got to git Cap'n Dodge!"

Though Ma wanted to send Dave to catch him a fresh horse, the horses were nowhere in sight and Ed Mansfield would not wait. "My hoss is rested some," he said. " 'T ain't far to Egeria Creek. We'll push on."

"Do you think the Indians will stand a fight?" Ma asked anxiously.

"I don't know, ma'am. I don't think so."

They watched him ride on up the valley, his horse stumbling a little.

"I wish Jimmy was home!" said Ma.

CHAPTER XIX

After Ed Mansfield had brought word that the Utes at White River Agency had started their war dance, the settlers were extremely uneasy. But, as Mr. Metcalf pointed out, the Agency was a long way off, and there did not seem to be an Indian on Bear River. The inhabitants of Steamboat Springs went on with their work, though they often looked down the trail, hardly knowing what they expected to see.

The afternoon of September 30 was quiet and lazy. The kitchen had been hot all day because Ma had kept the fire going to bake bread. Now the last loaves were out of the oven, and only a wisp of smoke drifted from the stovepipe. The women were sewing and visiting while the children played croquet.

"Your turn, Martha," said Logan, whacking a wild timothy with his mallet.

Martha took so long preparing that Lulie had time to pick a spray of purple aster and stick it through a buttonhole of her dress. She had time to sniff the bittersweet smell of dry cottonwood leaves.

"If I can just get through that wicket . . ." Martha screwed one eye shut to take careful aim.

She never made the shot. The pound of hoofs caused her to jerk up. A horse came in sight, its rider leaning low and whipping it at every gallop.

"Why, it's Papa!" cried Vada.

Logan scowled. "He oughtn't to whip that horse. He's already run it so hard it's all lathered."

"And there comes Albert!" squealed Addie.

"Maybe the Indians are after 'em!" Lulie's heart gave a thump.

They threw down their mallets and raced for the cabin.

The sound of galloping hoofs brought the womenfolks rushing out, and brought Captain Metcalf running from his cabin with his rifle.

"The Indians are upon us!" shouted Mr. Reid. "Everybody go to the woods!"

He jumped off his wheezing horse and almost fell because his legs were stiff from riding so far. He managed to stagger into the storeroom, grabbed a sack of flour, and started down into the willows with it.

"Did you see the Indians?" cried Ma. "How do you know?"

"Oh, my goodness!" gasped Mrs. Reid, gripping the stocking she had been darning.

Mrs. Metcalf stood there, her eyes big and black in her small white face.

Ma ran after Mr. Reid and caught his arm and shook it. "How do you know?" she demanded.

Dropping the sack of flour, he ran back to pick up another, so excited he could not talk. His face was as red as his whiskers.

Albert was scared, too, but he could talk. "There's been a f-fight over on Milk Creek," he panted. "Injuns killed Major Thornburgh and a lot of soldiers that was on their way to the Agency."

"Who told you?" snapped Captain Metcalf.

"Fella that escaped from the Injuns at Milk Creek. Come after Captain Dodge. He says flee for our lives. The Utes are driving the settlers this way. Nobody knows what's happened to Meeker. Massacred, likely."

"And Jimmy so far away!" moaned Ma.

Mr. Reid found his voice. "No time to lose!" he jabbered. "Everybody hide in the willows—in that old dry beaver ditch——"

"Take it easy, friend," Captain Metcalf advised. "That would be the worst place you could go." Captain Metcalf had been an army man and knew a considerable amount about strategy. "The redskins could shoot right down on you from that hill across the river."

Just then Ellis Clark came jogging in with the Hayden mail. The solid way he sat his saddle, and his unhurried manner, made everyone feel better.

"Did you see any Indians?" cried Lulie.

"No, but I saw a mighty bad scairt man," drawled Ellis, looking at Mr. Reid. "I was eatin' lunch at the halfway cabin with Bert Smart—he's been putting up hay there—when Reid come tearing up with word of Thornburgh's massacre. He wouldn't even eat."

"I don't blame him," said Mrs. Metcalf.

Mr. Reid, the sweat rolling off his face, was still carrying things down into the willows. The rest of them held a council of war right there in front of the cabin, with the sun slanting from the west and a few straggling robins scolding in the chokecherry bushes.

Ellis said, "I reckon that messenger, Ed Mansfield, reached Captain Dodge yesterday and Captain Dodge is cutting across Twenty Mile Park now on his way to the Agency. He doesn't know about the fight, but he soon will. Someone'll git word to him from Hayden."

Ma still wore her thimble on her finger. Her cheeks were flushed, her eyes very bright. "Jimmy told me if there was trouble to take the children and go up Soda Creek, and that's what I'm going to do," she declared.

Captain Metcalf nodded gravely. "Mrs. Metcalf will go with you. I'll stay around here a while and see what happens. Then I'll join you."

"Mike LeDuc isn't due with the mail from Rock Creek till tomorrow," said Ellis, "but I'll saddle a fresh horse and go meet him and spread the news."

"Ride fast," Ma begged, "and tell the mail carrier from Rock Creek to Hot Sulphur to get word to Mr. Crawford."

She sent Dave after the horses.

"Hope dey ain't away over on Elk River," he muttered as he struck off at a jog trot.

Ellis went with him. Mr. Metcalf had his horses picketed nearby. He saddled one while Mrs. Metcalf hurried to her cabin for her coat.

Ma worked quickly, as if she had it all planned. She dumped the baking of fresh bread into a flour sack. She lifted Pa's rifle from the deerhorn rack and filled a buckskin bag with ammunition.

"Lulie," she ordered, "get that old 'tarp' and roll up some blankets in it, and Logan, run to the storehouse and fetch that ham of venison."

In three quarters of an hour Dave came back, riding Chief and leading Puss and Monty. Luckily the horses had been grazing only a short distance up the gulch.

Ellis rode Coaly. He threw on his saddle and lost no time heading up the valley.

Dave saddled Chief and Puss and packed little Monty. Lulie helped him. They knotted the ropes as fast as they could, expecting any moment to hear an Indian war whoop. The sun was almost down; the shadows of the sagebrush were as long as pine trees. Ponto, eager for any kind of trip, jumped about the horses' heads, and Spy watched worriedly because she sensed something was wrong.

In the midst of all this, Lulie spied John running up the hill.

"John! Where are you going?" she cried.

"To hide my marble with the sheep in it," he flung back.

Reminded of her own treasures, Lulie rushed into the cabin, seized her autograph album, her paints and brushes, and the red lead pencil Grandma had sent her, and dashed up the hill where John had already poked his marble in a crack in the rocks. She shoved her possessions into a hollow under a shallow ledge; pulled the bushes together in front; and ran back to the cabin—only to remember the song book on the clock shelf. No Indian was going to get that! Snatching it, she tore down to the Bent Cottonwood and thrust it in the hole above the "organ." Now that the woodchucks were asleep, the hole was a dry, safe place, and she felt better not having all her valuables in one spot.

Breathless, she returned to the kitchen. "What else, Ma——"

Ma was not there—only Logan, who had remembered that salt was important and was tying up a handful in a rag. She ran into the bedroom, dark already because it was against the hill, and there was Ma on her knees.

"—and Father, take care of us," Ma whispered.

Quickly Ma rose to her feet and stood a moment, looking about. She had a little money hid back of the door casing, and she got that. Tommy Bantam, marching into the kitchen to roost, cocked a golden eye at her.

"Come, children," Ma said.

"Come, Tommy," cried Logan, swooping up the bantam.

But Tommy saw no sense in abandoning the comfortable room. He flew out of Logan's grasp to skip behind the flower stand where no one could reach him. Logan had to leave him, for Ma was already climbing onto her sidesaddle from the mounting rock.

It seemed strange and awful to be going away from home as night was falling—away from the warmth and security of their log cabin to the autumn chill of the woods. Even bundled in their coats, they shivered.

Dave hung back. "Miss Maggie," he protested, "if dere's gwine to be any fightin', I wants to be in it!" His old muzzle loader had no cartridges, but he clutched it fiercely. He wore his six-shooter strapped to his waist.

Ma shook her head. "You must come with us, Dave. We'll need you."

Mr. Metcalf had sent Mrs. Metcalf ahead, up the trail, on her horse. Now he boosted John behind Ma. "Mrs. Crawford," he said, "I'll come along the creek about midnight, and I'll whistle."

Ma told him about where she thought they would be, and loosened Chief's bridle reins. He led off. Lulie and Logan on Puss came next, and Dave walked behind, leading Monty.

Instead of following the creek, Ma took a short cut across the mesa to reach the stream higher up. As the little procession passed the henhouse, the geese set up a racket. No one had had time to shut the henhouse door. In the marsh a killdeer cried lonesomely. From the Reid camp Martha called a tearful good-by. She and her father and mother were dragging bedding into the dry beaver ditch, while Vada and Addie tried to coax their kitten down from a tree.

Lulie snatched a last look at the cabin before the hill hid it. *I may never see it again,* she thought despairingly. It appeared peaceful enough there in the sunset glow, with the woodpile near it, the grindstone sitting in the yard, and over all the Stars and Stripes, furled in the evening calm.

In a quarter of a mile they caught up with Mrs. Metcalf. Except for the tight way she gripped the bridle reins and the spark of excitement in her eyes, she might have been going for a pleasure ride.

Dusk gathered fast as they rode single file through the sagebrush. The horses, reluctant to go, took mincing steps till Ma cut Chief with the end of the bridle; then he lengthened out and reached Soda Creek while there was barely enough light to see the game trail down the steep bank. Lulie wished the horses' hoofs would not make so much noise on the gravel; wished Monty, behind her, would not grunt so when he had to cross a log. Any Indians within a mile could hear!

Ma let Chief pick the way through the willows and wild meadowland of Soda Park, where it was already night. Though branches slapped the riders and tore at their clothes, nobody said a word. Every stump looked like a crouched Indian! The horses knew better. They kept traveling.

Suddenly, against the western skyline, Lulie saw figures moving, one after another. Her heart came up to smother her tongue. She jabbed Logan with her elbow, and he clutched her tightly.

"Indians!" he gasped.

Then they heard the cowbell and almost laughed aloud. Their "Indians" were only the milk cows, trailing home to be milked. And there would be no one to milk them.

It seemed a hundred years since last June when Ma, Logan, John, and Lulie had ridden up this very trail to pick wild strawberries. Something crackling through the brush made the horses snort. A deer or elk, Lulie thought. She was not afraid of anything that made so much commotion.

They had covered perhaps a mile, with the horses stumbling over roots and into holes, when Ma stopped and the rest stopped behind her. As silently and quickly as they could, they tied the horses among the tall willows and hid the saddles and bridles in brush clumps. Not very far away the mountain was aglare with forest fire. A dim glow reached even here, making it possible for them to see how to cross the creek on rocks. They climbed a few steps up the hill and sat down in the deep shadow to wait.

In spite of the fire so near, the night was sharp, and they huddled together in blankets to try to keep warm. Back of them, against the orange sky, they could see the black spines of burned trees. They could hear the popping of flames, and now and then a crash when a tree went down. A coyote yipped on the opposite ridge—or was it an Indian? Tense and shivery, they tried to peer through the darkness.

All the bloody tales of Indian warfare Lulie had ever heard swarmed through her mind. She wondered if the

Utes had already attacked Steamboat Springs and toma-hawked the Reids and Mr. Metcalf.

"Ma——" she whispered.

"Sssh!" cautioned Ma, the rifle in her hands.

One arm around Spy, six-year-old John went to sleep, and pretty soon the blanket sagged and Logan was asleep in spite of himself.

Ma and Mrs. Metcalf and Lulie and Dave kept watch. The big red moon climbed over the mountain. It was almost full, and in its subdued light the valley below looked peaceful enough. Slowly it slid above the flames and smoke into the cool depth of the sky.

Lulie's foot went to sleep. When she stretched it out, she knocked loose a rock that bounced down the slope with a dreadful lot of noise. If Indians were around, they would surely hear it! Above the burble of the creek, Lulie tried to sort out the small rustlings of the night; tried to determine if among them was a stealthy footfall. Ponto, usually loud-mouthed, pressed against her, growling faintly. He was scared, too.

"Must be after midnight," whispered Mrs. Metcalf. "Why doesn't the Captain——"

"Dat moon say it only be about ten," said Dave.

"Sssh!" said Ma.

Lulie was sure the Indians had got Captain Metcalf. She had never been so cramped and tired and cold in her life. Nor so frightened. The smell of burning pine was so strong it almost made her sick.

Suddenly Dave spoke right out loud. "Miss Maggie, I heard a whistle. I knows I did!"

They strained to listen. Sure enough, in a minute they all heard it.

Mrs. Metcalf was on her feet. "It's the Captain!"

"Answer him, Dave," said Ma.

Dave whistled.

Now they could discern the figure of the Captain on the opposite bank. The creek made such a mumble it was hard to hear what he was trying to tell them, but Lulie was almost sure he said, "We've got to go on!"

CHAPTER XX

If Captain Metcalf thought they had to go on, that meant the Utes were in Steamboat Springs.

"Come, John! Logan!" Ma shook the boys awake.

Mrs. Metcalf had already run down the hill to meet her husband, who had now ridden across the creek. The rest of them slid and stumbled after her, Lulie dragging John by his small, cold fist. She thought how the Utes had always wanted him and Logan for their red hair.

"Hurry!" she gasped. "We've got to run from the Indians!"

But when they reached Mr. Metcalf, they learned that what he had really said was, "We have to go home!"

Gathered around him in the eerie glow from the forest fire, they heard him explain, "I've seen no Indians, and the settlers from Hayden have come to Steamboat. There are enough of us now to put up a fair fight if necessary. I think we had better go back to the cabin and fortify."

"I believe that's what Jimmy would advise," said Ma, relief in her voice.

What a time they had hunting the saddles and bridles they had hidden so well!

"Find 'em, Spy!" Ma urged. "Go find 'em, Ponto!"

"Here's one saddle," cried Logan.

They were not trying to be quiet any more.

Clawing through the grass, Mrs. Metcalf moaned, "I can't find my bridle! I don't know where I put it!"

Lulie remembered hiding her things under a big root, and after snagging her arms on the gooseberry bushes that grew thick everywhere among the willows, she finally found them. When she rushed up to Puss with the bridle, the mare snorted in her face.

"Whoa, Puss! Whoa, girl! We're going home!"

Puss's eyes glowed like a cat's. Her nose was as cold as Lulie's.

How much better to be going home than into those big mountains! thought Lulie as she worked the bit between the mare's teeth. It had been so easy to pull the saddles off, and it was so much trouble to get them on again! Cinches kinked, and straps would not go through buckles. Mrs. Metcalf never did locate her bridle. She had to ride with only a halter to guide by.

Anyway, the horses needed no guiding. They were more than glad to go home. Dave rode with Logan, and Lulie behind Captain Metcalf, while Monty trotted along by himself with the pack. It seemed no distance at all back to Steamboat Springs—to the familiar muffled rush of Bear River and to the moonlit shapes of corral and cabin.

As the riders crossed the sagebrush and came down over the little hill, they could see the wagons standing in front of the cabin plainly. A horse whinnied. The Captain's horse answered.

"There's no light in the window," whispered Lulie.

"Those folks are afraid to make a light," said the Captain.

He gave a low whistle, and a man with a gun stepped out from the shadow of some bushes.

"All quiet so far, Captain," the man reported. "That you, Mrs. Crawford? Bert Smart from Hayden. You'll find your cabin full of folks. We thought this was the best place to come."

"I'm glad you did, Mr. Smart," Ma told him.

The cabin was indeed full of folks. Most of the men were outdoors, on guard at various points, but the women and children huddled in the dark log rooms, talking in low voices. All of Hayden had come—Mr. and Mrs. Smart and their boy, Gordy; Mr. and Mrs. Marshall and Mrs. Thompson. (Mr. Thompson was in Denver.) Two young men from Below, Zene Maudlin and Jimmy Norton, had come with the Hayden people. Mr. and Mrs. Farnsworth from Elk River were there. The Reids had abandoned their beaver ditch and joined the others.

All were relieved to see Ma.

"We put the post office in the wagon, grabbed what else we could, and came through Twenty Mile Park," said Mrs. Smart.

"The horses lost the road and it was dreadful bumping over sagebrush in that wagon," said Mrs. Marshall. "I'm nearly dead."

"We didn't dare wait till morning," quavered Mrs. Thompson. "The messenger said the Indians were coming, and to flee for our lives."

Quietly Ma took charge. The first thing she did was make a fire and start to cook. None of the visitors had taken time to eat before they came.

Mrs. Metcalf lighted the lamp, after tacking blankets over the windows so that if Indians were watching they could not see the people moving in the house. She turned the wick low and set the lamp back where it could not shine through any cracks.

Somebody had milked the cows. The children drank the warm milk, ate the venison Ma set on the table, and sopped their bread in the gravy. The bread had been up Soda Creek and back and was molded to the shape of the pack saddle, but nobody cared. Poor Mrs. Marshall could not eat a bite. She sat by the stove, her head in her hands. Ma did not eat, either, though she kept working.

The men tramped in, one or two at a time, and ate heartily.

"Oh, I wonder if Nannie and Henry are safe," worried Ma.

Jimmy Norton said, "Mrs. Crawford, if you'll furnish a horse, I'll ride up to Hahn's Peak and see."

"Take Chief," Ma said quickly. "He can follow any trail in the dark."

Jimmy Norton buttoned his coat, settled his hat against the frosty night, and struck out.

The men arranged to take turns standing guard.

Ma put her visitors in the beds as far as the beds would go, and the rest of the folks slept on the floor. In a corner of the back room Lulie, Martha, Vada, and Addie shivered together under one quilt. Even with all their clothes on, they were cold, and the floor was very hard. They lay whispering, too excited to sleep, fearing any minute the Indians might attack.

During the night Lulie heard men tramp in and out as they changed the guard, but Captain Metcalf would not give up his place by the west window to anyone. He sat there with his rifle till daybreak.

Next morning, rumpled and heavy-eyed, the people in the cabin peered out at October sunshine. Lulie, stepping down the back trail to empty a pan of water, could have believed she had dreamed a bad dream if it had not been for the clutter of wagons, the extra horses in the corral, and two or three strange dogs running about. The cottonwoods still stood golden by the river, and Elk Mountain stretched serene and gray across the west.

As Ma cooked breakfast, she ventured, "We're so far from Milk Creek and the Agency, surely the Indians wouldn't——"

"Now that they've smelled blood," growled Mr. Reid, his red chin whiskers abristle, "they're sure to send war parties up Snake River and Bear River."

" 'T ain't far on a fast hoss," said Mr. Smart. "And the Utes have got plenty of hosses."

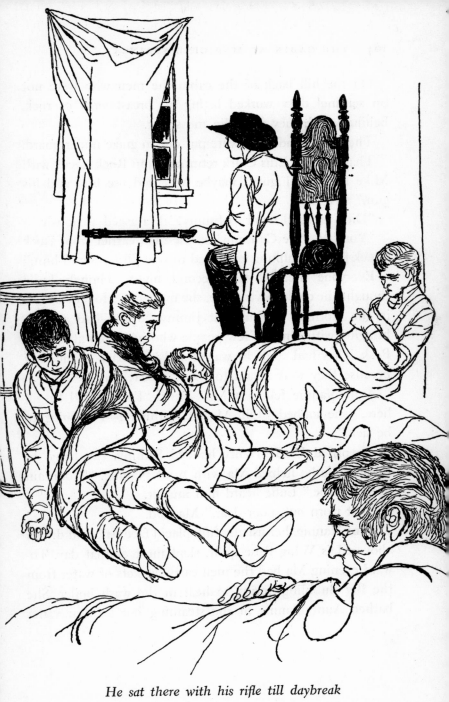

He sat there with his rifle till daybreak

On the hill back of the cabin the men who were not on sentinel duty worked laying up breastworks of rock, behind which they could lie and shoot.

The horses and cows were put out to graze under guard.

That evening Ellis Clark returned from Rock Creek with Mike LeDuc. "Figured maybe we could use him and his gun," said Ellis.

"Did you send word to Jimmy?" Ma asked anxiously.

"You bet. Arie Cantonwine, the mail carrier from Rock Creek to Hot Sulphur, promised to ride till he found him."

Everyone dreaded that second night. Though Lulie thought she could never sleep, she must have, for she awoke in the morning to find that Jimmy Norton had arrived, bringing with him the few people who had been at Hahn's Peak. They had come by wagon and horseback in the dark because they were afraid to travel in daylight.

Aunt Nannie fell into Ma's arms. "I'm so glad to get here," she sobbed. "Oh, Maggie, I think I—I'm going to be sick."

A worried Uncle Henry handed Sammy, the baby, to Lulie while he helped Ma with Aunt Nannie. "Mountain fever, maybe," Lulie heard him mutter.

"Just worn out, poor dear," Ma said.

Aunt Nannie, her usually full, placid face pale and drawn above Ma's Whig Rose quilt, slept most of that day. Toward evening Ma had the men carry buckets of water from the Big Bubbling Spring to heat in the wash boiler. She bathed Aunt Nannie in the steaming hot sulphur water till the sick woman complained she was parboiled. By morning Aunt Nannie was better.

Meanwhile, Lulie and Martha took care of the good-natured Sammy, with Vada and Addie begging to hold him because he was more fun than their rag dolls.

After a day or two of having to stay in the cabin, or what Ma called "the yard," the children could not find anything to do that was much fun. They had played tick-tacktoe and guess-where-I'm-hiding and everything they could think of, and they had told riddles and tales till they had nothing more to tell. Though they begged to go down to the flat and play croquet, or go fishing—"just to the mouth of Soda Creek"—the grown folks would not let them.

"And Indian could sneak along the creek in the willows as easy as not," Ma said.

"The Indians wouldn't hurt us," John pouted. "We never did anything to them."

Lulie was not so sure. "Look what happened to Abraham Elliott in Middle Park last year. He never did anything to the Indians either, and he got shot in the back to get even for what someone else did."

"Wonder if Charlie Yarmonite is doing a war dance," mused Logan. "If he is, I'd sure like to see him."

"Yarmonite wouldn't let anyone hurt us," John maintained stubbornly. "He's our friend."

"Yarmonite's only one Indian," sighed Lulie. "There are lots of others." She was thinking especially of Piah and Colorow. The thought was not comforting.

When Ma had had time to count noses, she missed two of her neighbors. "Has anybody seen Uncle Tow or Trader Shouse?" she asked.

"A week or ten days ago Uncle Tow was up at the Peak," remembered Uncle Henry. "He was wantin' to know how to play Canute."

"Why, that's the game Trader Shouse was teaching him last spring," exclaimed Lulie.

"And I'll warrant Shouse won everything the old man had," snorted Uncle Henry. "That trader is crooked as a dog's hind leg."

"Poor old Uncle Tow," said Mrs. Reid. "I hope the Utes haven't got his scalp."

"Where do you reckon Shouse is?" asked Uncle Henry.

"On his way to Denver, I expect," said Lulie.

Maybe he was already in Denver at the land office, making the payment Pa had hoped to make. He must be rich after his summer's "take" of gold dust, ponies, and buckskin. Pa never would get to Denver now, and the land office would give Shouse first right to Steamboat Springs. It had been one thing after another all summer—the money lost in the river, the survey delayed by forest fires, and now this. *'T isn't fair!* Lulie thought rebelliously, and was glad when Ma sent her to the storehouse for dried apples, because then no one would see the tears rolling down her cheeks.

Sometime during the night of October 2 the people in the cabin heard a commotion outside.

"Indians!" gasped Martha, clutching Lulie.

The guards had given no warning. Ma opened the door a crack, then flung it wide and threw her arms around the big figure standing there.

"Jimmy!" she cried.

The mail carrier, Pa said, had caught up with him near the head of Middle Park and, though it was near midnight, Pa had immediately started home. He had left his wagon and team at a ranch; borrowed a fast horse; and about daybreak had reached Hot Sulphur Springs, where five men had volunteered to come with him to fight Indians.

"We didn't know what we'd find," Pa said, "but when we came close enough to see the corral in the moonlight, and the cows lying down chewing their cuds, we knew everything must be all right."

The men wanted Pa to take charge. The first thing he did next morning was to send Lem Farnsworth and Ed Hodges down the river, with instructions to keep going till they found out the danger from the Indians. Then he began to dig a pit between the cabin and Soda Creek so that the people could go there as a last resort if the cabin was fired by burning arrows. When it was finished, the cellar was circular with a dirt-covered roof just above the ground, under which were portholes on every side. A tunnel connected it with the house. If need be, Pa said, another tunnel could be dug to the creek for water. In this cellar he stored some food.

There was precious little food left to store. Ma had been

feeding most of Routt County for an endless number of days. In their haste to flee from the Indians, the settlers had not brought fifty pounds of provisions among them. Ma's larder had been low anyhow because it was the end of summer and Pa had not hauled in the winter's supplies. He had not even hauled in the second load on which he had planned last June. Fortunately he had hung three deer on the back of the cabin several days before he had started Outside with the surveyors. Now the venison was almost gone.

That was why Logan was so excited one morning when he went for a pail of water. The children were allowed to go the few steps to the creek just above the footlog.

"Lulie!" he shouted. "John! Come here! Quick!"

They ran to see what was the matter.

Soda Creek was flopping full of fish! Logan, astraddle of some rocks, was throwing them out with his hands. He already had his bucket full.

"Look at the grayling!" he yelled. "There's millions of 'em! Somebody bring a tub!"

The silvery fish were squirming and wriggling in the shallows among the rocks.

"I caught one!" squealed Vada.

It was no trick at all to catch them. The fishermen did not even have to get their feet wet. They soon had the tub full, and some of the men carried it to the cabin.

"Those grayling must be running up the streams to spawn," said Pa.

How good they tasted, fried crisp and brown!

"As good as trout," Lulie declared.

"Just when we needed them," said Ma. "It's providential."

Everyone had all he could eat, and Ma salted down a tubful.

A week had passed, and nothing had happened, and the people crowded in the cabin were becoming restless. They had had no news from Outside, no further word from Below. This was the fat of the year, just before the lean, cold winter, and they should be picking the wild fruit that still hung dead ripe on the bushes. They should be getting some of those deer that were rolling out of the higher mountains and drifting toward lower country. They should be chinking their cabins and driving their stock to winter range. One of these days snow would come, and this time it would be welcome because it would put out the forest fires.

"I don't believe there are any Indians around," stated Mrs. Reid one evening.

"Come over here," Ma said quietly, "and look out this window." She pushed aside the blanket curtain.

On a ridge across the river not far from the bluff a stab of light pierced the dusk.

"I didn't know the forest fires had spread down there," exclaimed Mrs. Reid.

"I don't believe that's a forest fire," said Ma. "See, now it's gone."

"It comes and goes," observed John. "Ma, what is it?"

Ma did not answer till the stab of fire had come and gone twice more.

"What is it, Ma?" asked John.

"I think," she said, "it's an Indian signal fire."

CHAPTER XXI

Signal fire!

The words flashed through the cabin. The watchers at the windows talked in low, frightened tones. Vada and Addie hid behind the woodbox.

Pa had seen the signal, too. When he came in, his face was grave. "Some Indian sending a message," he said.

"What do you think it meant, Pa?" asked Lulie.

"Wish I knew. It could be seen a long way down river."

"Mike and I thought the Indians were around," Ellis Clark said. "While we were guarding the stock yesterday, we heard some hosses splash through the creek above us. Nothing goes through a creek quite like a hoss. I tell you, we let out our lariats and rounded up our critters in a hurry. Smoke was so thick we couldn't see, but I'm willing to bet Indians were after our herd."

"And I saw a fresh pony track on the hill yonder," put in Zene Maudlin. "I know it was Injun."

"How do you know?" asked Mrs. Metcalf.

"It was unshod. All our hosses is shod."

"A Ute scout looking us over," shivered Martha.

The uneasy settlers doubled their precautions, but nothing happened that night, nor the next, nor all that week, and they saw no more signal fires.

By that time Lem Farnsworth and Ed Hodges, the men Pa had sent Below, were back. They had traveled as far as Lay Creek where they had met troop reinforcements on their way from Rawlins to the scene of the trouble. A scout named Joe Rankin had managed to slip out of the rifle pits at Milk Creek the same time as the messenger who had come up Bear River. Joe had made it to Rawlins and spread the alarm.

"From what the soldiers told us," said Ed Hodges, "there isn't much left of the White River Agency. Them red devils burned the buildings, massacred all the employees, and stuck a barrel stave through Meeker's mouth. And then they took the three white women and two white children captive."

Mrs. Reid shuddered. "Just think, it might have happened to us!"

"I'll always believe we owe our lives to Yarmonite," Ma declared, peering out the window as though she could see the Ute chief standing there now. "I think Yarmonite was truly our friend. I think he has been afraid of trouble all summer. Remember, weeks ago, how he said, 'Mebbeso Big Jim take his squaw and papooses, and Yarmonite take his squaw and papooses and go Denber City'? I don't believe he wanted to fight."

"I guess when the time came, he had to stick with his people," Lulie added thoughtfully.

1

"Might be," said Ed. "The soldiers claim he shot more hosses at Milk Creek than any other Ute, though I dunno how they know."

"What became of Sandy and Captain Dodge and the Negro soldiers?" asked Logan.

"Rode all night to reach Milk Creek," answered Lem Farnsworth. "Jumped into the rifle pits with what was left of Thornburgh's command, and defended 'em against the Indians till Merritt's men got there three days later."

The listeners were gravely silent, contemplating this act of courage that was to be recorded as one of the bravest deeds in Western history.

"Those were the soldiers we saw," said John, awed. "Sandy'll tell us all about it some day."

Grimly Lem continued, "Them Indians fired from ambush. Major Thornburgh was among the first to fall. Twelve of his men were killed and forty-two wounded. The rest dug in behind the wagons and the bodies of the horses. They were there five days."

"Five days!" exclaimed Pa. "I bet it seemed like five weeks to those men—most of 'em wounded. The stench from the dead horses must have been fierce. Do you know where the Indians are now, Lem?"

"We was told they'd all fled to the Uncompahgre country. Ouray, the head chief, had sent a messenger from Los Pinos Agency and ordered 'em to quit fightin'. Ouray is a friend of the white men. Anyhow, there was too many soldiers swarmin' in."

"You sure there ain't some war parties still sneakin' around?" asked Mr. Reid.

Lem shrugged. "If we was in the lower valley, there might be some danger, but here——" He cocked an eye at the gray sky. "Goin' to snow any day, no telling how deep. It's my notion even fool young braves wouldn't risk gittin' in snow where their horses couldn't travel. Reckon the danger on Bear River is over till next spring."

"I better hit for Rock Creek with the mail," said Mike LeDuc. "Folks Outside'll be mighty worried to hear."

Those who had relatives scrawled hasty messages for Mike to take, and then, anxious to learn whether their cabins had been molested, hitched up and headed home— all except Uncle Henry's family, which had decided to stay in Steamboat Springs, and Zene Maudlin and Jimmy Norton, who pitched in to help Uncle Henry round up the stock and drive them to winter range in Burns's Hole, some forty miles south. Only Lil, a white cow, was left bawling in the corral to eat from the small haystack and to furnish milk for the family.

The Reids departed with the Hayden people—Martha, Vada, and Addie reluctant, and turning to wave till they were out of sight. In spite of the anxiety and discomforts, the children had had almost the best time they could remember. *We'll write every mail!* Lulie and Martha had promised each other.

Lulie, Logan, and John listened to the joggle of wagon wheels die away. They stood taking great gulps of the salty mineral air, stretching arms and legs like chickens that had sat too long on a roost.

"Race you to the Iron Spring!" cried Logan.

Pell-mell, they plunged to the Iron Spring and beyond to the Big Bubbling Spring and on to the pond and back up on the rocks. How good to run again! And that night, how good to sleep in their own beds!

Captain and Mrs. Metcalf were all packed and ready to travel, but were waiting to go out when Pa did.

Now that the Indian trouble appeared to be over on Bear River, at least for the winter, Pa thought of the team and wagon he had left in Middle Park and of the urgent errand upon which he had started weeks ago.

"Trader Shouse has had plenty of time to beat me to the land office," he said ruefully.

"The whelp!" growled Uncle Henry. He glanced at Pa uncertainly. "But if he has, Jim, there must be lots of other good land to file on."

"There's no other Steamboat Springs!"

"Oh, Pa," wailed Lulie, "what will we do?"

"Well, we won't holler till we're hurt," was Pa's gruff reply. "We don't know for sure what Shouse has done, and we won't know till I reach Denver. And I can't go to Denver till I do a few things here."

It was almost November. The storehouse was empty; the meat hooks on the back of the cabin were bare. Any time snow might come, so deep a horse could not travel. Pa found a herd of elk in the frosted brake ferns at the base of

Storm Mountain, and shot eight. He would pack his spare wagon with the best "saddles" or quarters of meat to take to Georgetown and sell to the hotels and restaurants so he would have money enough to buy the "substantials"—flour, meal, sugar, salt, bacon, molasses, and coffee. Dave was going with Pa to drive the team and wagon Pa had left in Middle Park.

The two of them hauled in the elk and dressed them out as fast as they could, working in the cold, clean grass a short distance up Soda Creek. The wind had the smell of snow in it, and the clouds over the range were like wrinkled gray flannel. Where smoke from the forest fires ended and clouds began was hard to tell.

Before it stormed, Lulie and John went to retrieve the treasures they had hidden in the rocks. They found the pencil and paint brushes and Lulie's album, and after considerable searching, John's marble with the sheep in it.

Remembering the hymn book, Lulie hurried down to the Bent Cottonwood. The roar of the river had subsided to a mumble, and the water, reflecting the dismal sky, looked cold and gray. A few yellow cottonwood leaves eddied against the broken tree branches that still swished back and forth in the current. Except for the snags, it was a good place to fish, and Lulie took time to peer intently into the clear depths. She could see long, shadowy shapes of trout pointed upstream. One was a monster! She would get the hymn book and then run home and bring her fishing pole.

Thrusting her hand into the hollow of the tree, which was deep and filled with loose bits of rotten wood, she felt around and pulled out the book—and something else.

For a minute she stood turning the second object in her hand, too amazed to think. It was an oblong, squarish packet of paper, yellowed and crinkled from having been in water. A blur of ink across the face gave evidence that there had once been writing on it. One corner had been chewed by mice or woodchucks, and through the ragged opening she could glimpse something inside that sent her racing for the cabin, shouting, "Ma! Pa! Look!"

Pa, who was painstakingly particular about care of meat, was so occupied that he paid no attention till she seized the dinner bell and rang it. That emergency signal brought him in startled bounds.

Ma was equally alarmed. "Lulie! What in creation——"

Logan and John came running.

"I've found it! I know that's it——"

"What?" cried John.

"In the hole in the Bent Cottonwood——" Lulie's words tumbled over each other. "Look, Pa!"

Pa, who had expected the house to be afire or Logan to have chopped his foot, took the packet, frowning, and then abruptly reached for his pocketknife and slit the brittle paper. So intent was he that he seemed to have stopped breathing.

The family looked on, hardly believing what they saw. In Pa's hand lay brownish-black pieces of paper with figures and printing on them. Lulie, leaning close, could make out the words.

"Silver Certificate," she pronounced.

"Silver Certificate," echoed Ma. "Why, that's money! Oh, Jimmy, it must be——"

"Uncle Hammond's money!" shouted Logan.

"That's what it is," Pa said in an awed voice. "Yessiree-bobtail Peter horsefly!"

He spread the battered bills upon the table, gently prying them apart. "Uncle Hammond's money," he repeated. "Twelve hundred dollars."

"Is it all there, Jimmy?" whispered Ma.

"It's all here—just a little the worse for wear!"

They touched it wonderingly.

"How did it get in the tree?" puzzled Logan.

Nobody knew. Pa, examining the ragged scalloping of teeth marks, said, "A woodchuck's been chewing it."

Together they pieced out an explanation.

"After the envelope was lost from the mail sack," Ma conjectured, "it must have washed against those dead cottonwood branches that drag in the water. And it must have been where a woodchuck could reach it."

"I expect Mrs. Woodchuck thought it was good to eat," suggested John.

"Or maybe she wanted it for bedding," said Logan. "Woodchucks are always carrying something in their mouths."

"If I hadn't been hunting for my book——" said Lulie.

"Uncle Hammond's money," marveled Pa. "After all this time! It was there high and dry while I was wading the river and breaking my neck to search the drift piles."

"Let me see it again," breathed Ma. "It's the greatest wonder in the world Lulie ever found it."

"I'm mighty glad she did!"

"Hurry, Pa! Hurry to the land office," cried Lulie. "Maybe it isn't too late!"

*

The morning Pa and Dave and Captain and Mrs. Metcalf drove away from Steamboat Springs a cold drizzle was falling.

Ma could hardly bear to part with Mrs. Metcalf.

"I don't suppose you'll ever want to come back after all this trouble," she sighed.

"Oh, we'll be back!" The Vermont Congressman's daughter nodded her head so vigorously that her old summer hat gave a flop. Her dark eyes sparkled beneath the limp brim. She hugged and kissed Ma. "Just look how well and strong the Captain is! And I've truly had a wonderful time! Wild horses couldn't keep us away, or wild Indians, either!"

CHAPTER XXII

The weather cleared in a hard freeze that brought the last cottonwood leaves spearing down to float golden in the dark backwash of river and creek. The storm had put out the forest fires, except for a wisp of smoke here and there. Most of Storm Mountain was an ugly black, but a few islands of pines remained. Lower down, where the blaze had not reached, the aspen groves stood naked. And here in the valley, frost had splashed the marsh grass with red as if a wounded deer had run through it.

Most of the deer had drifted to lower country, as dozens of heart-shaped tracks showed. Fleet and Fanny lay on the soft dirt of the dugout, big ears pointed west.

"One of these nights they'll be joining their wild cousins," Ma said. "I think Nature is telling them it is time to go."

She tied strips of red flannel around their necks so that hunters would know they were tame deer. They shivered their skins trying to shake off the new collars. The very next morning the round depressions where they had slept were there on the dugout, but Fleet and Fanny were gone.

Now that Aunt Nannie was feeling better, she and Sammy moved into their own cabin east of Soda Creek.

They came to the big cabin often, and Ma and the children visited Aunt Nannie a dozen times a day.

Uncle Henry would have to stay with the stock in Burns's Hole part of the winter. When Pa and Dave came back, they would take their turns.

After all the company and excitement of the last few weeks, the inhabitants of Steamboat Springs were keenly lonesome. Moreover, Ma was still apprehensive about Indians. She would not let the children go far from the cabin.

"I can't help feeling that Piah or some of his kind may sneak back to do more meanness," she said.

Though Logan and John had forgotten they were ever afraid, Lulie shared Ma's uneasiness. She kept close track of her brothers and often took time to scan the hills and valley with alert eyes. She saw no human movement, but every day ducks lifted from the pond with a noisy swish and did not return. Sandhill cranes trailed long legs across the sky, and down the wind came the sound of "honkers." Speckle's geese turned their heads sideways to listen. They were grown now, and their baby fuzz had been replaced by gray and white plumage; their necks were glossy black, topped by neat white ties. They ran down the trail, and sprang into the air with eager answers, beating their strong young wings. They rose easily, the biggest in the lead.

John, racing with them as far as he could, shrilled, "Good-by! Good-by!"

The wild geese circled as the youngsters caught up. Then

the leader swung the flock back on course, and the thin black V sketched rapidly through the clouds and was gone.

Killdeer swirled from the marsh in swift, low flight. They dipped once to the springs across the river, their cries shredding back before they were swallowed in the distance.

The pond was dull pewter under the November sky, except where a muskrat disturbed it. Any day now the muskrats and beaver would retire to their snug homes of sticks, mud, and reeds.

Even the dogs had gone with the horses and cattle. They were not there to answer the coyotes and foxes that raised a lively chorus every night or the great gray wolves that sometimes howled even in daylight.

Tobe and Tabby, the big gray cats that had lived on Lookout Mountain all summer, sleeping in a hole on the rocky knoll the children called "Tobe's Hill," came slipping around the warm cabin; but for a long time they were so wild, they were afraid to come in. The children coaxed them with pans of milk, and finally the cats streaked into the kitchen to hide behind the stove. In a few days they became as tame as before.

Ma and the children did the best they could to prepare for winter. They redaubed the cabin with white mineral clay, and dragged in all the dead wood they could find nearby. They fished at the mouth of Soda Creek almost every day. Though the fish were not biting much, and the children soon tired of throwing their hooks into the slow, dark water, Ma fished patiently. She smoked and salted the trout she caught, and added them to the slender food supply. The storehouse was emptier than it had been last spring, except that Ma had packed two big earthenware jars with butter and cottage cheese before the cows had been driven to winter range. There was a sack of dried serviceberries, and there was plenty of meat, but there was no flour, meal, or sugar.

"Hope Pa doesn't forget to bring a keg of Honey-Drip Syrup," Logan said wistfully.

Last spring they had waited and watched for Pa, and now they waited and watched with a sharper anxiety, knowing he had to make the trip back across the high mountain passes before the winter storms began. He and Dave had been gone more than two weeks. The children spent half their time climbing to the roof to peer up the valley. All they saw was the wind bending the willows. They wondered—oh, how they wondered—what had happened at the land office!

One afternoon John, who had gone to look at his mink traps, came running in, excited. Lulie's first thought was that he had seen Pa coming. But John cried, "It's Uncle Tow! It's Uncle Tow! And he's got four horses!"

Ma also must have thought Pa was coming. She was tired and disappointed, and her patience snapped. "John," she reproved severely, "you're old enough to know better. I've told you over and over—everything is not four! Go bring me a switch."

"But he *has* got four horses!" John insisted.

"You betcha!" Uncle Tow himself materialized in the doorway. "And two-three weeks ago I had forty hosses!"

Ma looked startled. People who lived alone too much sometimes turned queer. She peered at him doubtfully. Same gnarly figure. Same lean, leathery face with its frost of gray whiskers. The only things different about him were a new hat and a gorgeous new red-checked wool shirt.

"Forty hosses," he repeated, his old eyes sparkling. "I sold most of 'em in Georgetown, along with the buckskin and blankets and stuff."

"Why—why, Uncle Tow—" Ma stammered, "I'm so glad you're safe! I was afraid maybe the Indians——"

"Shucks, no! Me and Trader Shouse was playin' Canute."

"Shouse!" echoed Lulie. "Why, I thought he——"

"I shore learnt how to play Canute," chuckled the mountain man. "You recollect the game—you bury a stick in the sand, and t'other player guesses which mound it's in. Feller at Hahn's Peak told me that big ring Shouse wore was rigged out with a small magnetic needle. Shouse seen to it the stick had a nail in it. Course, the needle pointed to the nail. 'T warn't hard fer him to locate that stick."

"The big cheat!" cried Logan, who had rushed in from chopping wood to hear the prospector's tale, Tommy on his shoulder.

"Shouse, he was purty near through Middle Park when I caught up with him," continued Uncle Tow. "He shore wasn't anxious to play Canute. But," he added with a wrin-

kled grin, indicating the gun in his saddle holster, "he did!
This time I borrowed his ring, and you know something? I
won every time." He ruminated a minute. "Shucks, I'd have
let him keep some of that truck he took from the Injuns and
two-three hosses if he hadn't treated Podge so mean."

Podge was dozing by the Warm Iron Spring. When the
other horses came near, he laid back his ears and kicked at
them.

"Podge, he ain't changed," said the old man affection-
ately. "He's the meanest hoss!"

"Then I bet Trader Shouse never went to the land office,"
cried Logan, "because he wouldn't have any money."

"If that's so——" Ma began, a glow of excitement coming
in her cheeks.

"—why then Pa could make his deposit and we won't
lose Steamboat Springs!" Lulie finished breathlessly.

The wonder of what they had just learned held them
spellbound till John broke in. "Ma, I *told* you Uncle Tow
had four horses!"

Ma gave the back of John's jeans a gentle smack. "Son,"
she said, "I'm glad you've finally learned to count."

"Well, I'll be gittin' on afore it storms," remarked the
visitor, starting for his horses.

"Let me fix you something to eat," insisted Ma.

"Thankee, but I better hit for my 'hole.' " The old man
waved a stump of a pipe at the clouds. "Snow's a-comin',
shore enough."

"Wait a minute, Uncle Tow," called Lulie. "I want to

ask you something. Did Trader Shouse really build that cabin near the cave?"

"Him?" The prospector stiffened with scorn. "That cabin was thar years afore Shouse come to this country. Reckon some fur trappers built it."

He paused to stare across the river. His happy mood fell away, leaving him old and shrunken. His eyes grew bleak. "Times is changin'," he muttered. "Ain't a handful of mountain men left. And now the Injuns is gone, too."

"Won't they be back next summer?" asked Logan. "I broke my hunting bow and I wish Yarmonite would make me another."

"Don't reckon the government'll let the Utes hunt and camp in these mountains any more."

"Won't we ever see Yarmonite again?" John cried, unbelieving.

"Or Charlie?" added Logan anxiously.

Uncle Tow chewed his pipe. "Tha's talk of herdin' all the Utes out of Colorado."

"It would be a real relief not to have Indians around," Ma admitted, "though I can't help feeling sorry for them."

Lulie guessed Ma was thinking of all the biscuits she had had to bake for them and of the times Colorow and Piah had tried to scare her.

"Don't seem fair to punish the whole bunch," Uncle Tow growled. "Shore, they've killed white men, but this here trouble wasn't all their fault. Meeker, he didn't savvy Injuns."

Lulie said soberly, "I guess the Utes owned these mountains long before the white men came."

"Some of 'em was the best friends a man ever had!" Uncle Tow's lean jaw quivered. Abruptly he climbed on his horse. Podge bowed his spine in a halfhearted buck before he started up the trail toward Elk River. Ordinarily the old man would have chuckled at this show of spirit; now he humped lonesomely in the saddle, and did not even seem aware of his "winnings," trotting along on a pack string behind him.

Lulie looked at the sagebrush mesa where she had watched Indian campfires twinkle so often. She tried to think how she would feel if she were an Indian and could never, never return to Medicine Springs.

Ma said matter-of-factly, "Uncle Tow doesn't know for sure what's going to be done about the Indians. I don't believe anybody knows yet. Your Pa may have some news when he comes. And I wish he would come! It's going to snow, and how will he and Dave ever get those heavy wagons home!"

*

It was a sober family that watched the storm swirl nearer and nearer down the scarred black slopes of the range. They knew the road from Georgetown was only a trail, dangerous enough in dry weather, almost impassable when hills and rocks were slick and creeks icy. What if Pa and Dave never got home?

It was almost dusk when the first hard, white pellets hit the valley. Lulie, on her way to the Iron Spring to fill the jug, paused to squint at the hill with a frown.

Looks almost like campfire smoke yonder, she thought. *But it can't be! It's just the snow.*

An odd feeling came over her that someone or something was watching her. She made herself go on and fill the jug. Though she wanted to run to the cabin, she made herself walk. Pooh! There was nothing yonder except plumes of sagebrush, whipping in the wind! She did not say anything to anyone about her strange feeling.

She soon forgot about it herself, for through the storm came Pa's halloo, long and loud, with a *hoo-oo-OOT!* at the end. That was the most welcome sound the family had ever heard! Wagon wheels grated over the rocks of Soda Creek. The weary, frozen travelers were home!

The family rushed to greet them. One look at Pa's face was enough to tell them his trip had been successful.

"You paid the money at the land office," cried Lulie, "and Steamboat Springs is going to be ours!"

"Yessireebobtail Peter horsefly!" exulted Pa. "It was really the white duck pants that did it. I walked into the land office and the chief clerk said, 'Mr. Crawford, who is your tailor? I must have some pants like those.' "

"Jimmy, quit your blarneying," scolded Ma, delighted.

"Where's the other wagon?" Logan wanted to know.

"Had to hitch both teams to this one to haul it across

the river," said Pa. "We'll leave the other wagon on the far bank till morning. Can't take any risks with that load."

"What's in it?" asked John, dancing about.

Pa would not tell.

Through the dusk and the snow they could see it sitting over there, and thought they could see something big in the back.

"A stove," guessed John, "but we already have a stove."

"A dresser, maybe," guessed Ma, "or a cabinet."

Lulie did not dare say what was in her mind.

Later, as they all stood around the kitchen stove to warm, Lulie told Pa what Uncle Tow had said about the Indians. "Will the Utes really have to leave the mountains forever?" she asked.

"That's what the newspapers have been hollering for a long time," Pa said, frowning. "I guess it was bound to come sooner or later. Civilization is pushing into the last frontiers, and the Indians have to give way. It'll be easier for the homesteaders not to have redskins bothering around, but I can see the Utes' side, too. These were their mountains first."

"Where will the Utes go, Pa?"

"Somewhere west into country no white man wants." Pa jabbed another stick of wood into the stove. "Wish I could talk to old Yarmonite!"

He opened the door and peered out anxiously at the storm. "Soon as we get that other wagon forded, we'll have to hustle the teams to Burns's Hole. There's not enough hay for them here. They'd starve."

Lulie slept fitfully that night. Once she heard something *thump*, and thought it was a fox jumping from the hill onto the kitchen roof and trying to get at the meat.

Next morning Pa and Dave hauled the second wagon across the river. Fortunately the snow had not amounted to much. The horses slipped and grunted, and finally the wagon stood in front of the cabin.

When Pa removed the heavy tarpaulin and the oilcloth wrappings from the object in the back, Lulie was right!

"It's an organ!" shrilled John.

"Got it here without breaking it," Pa boasted. "Didn't tip over once!"

He looked straight at Lulie. He said, "I thought a little girl who tried to make music on an old cottonwood log ought to have an organ."

"Oh, Pa——" Lulie flung her arms around him. Something caught in her throat so she could not say another word.

"There, there now," Pa said gruffly, patting her. "Let's see if we can get this contraption unloaded."

Lulie watched Pa and Dave lift the organ out of the wagon and carry it into the cabin.

"Sho' must be a heap o' music in it, it's so heavy," puffed Dave.

"Solid walnut," said Pa. "The Metcalfs helped me make arrangements to get it."

"Put it here," Ma directed, "against this west wall."

Lulie did not know that the wind was blowing through the door or that she was shivering. She touched the beautiful wood. A real organ! Her organ! It had two side shelves and a tall carved top with a square frame in the middle. *For a mirror, or a vase,* she thought. The music rack lifted up, and deep inside was room to store music. Through the lacework of carving beneath the keyboard peeped a background of dark green cambric.

She raised the wooden cover, and there were the black and ivory keys waiting to be struck. She touched the gold letters that spelled *Burdett Organ* across the front, and examined the eight little round knobs, or "stops," that she knew could be pulled out to make different kinds of tones. Wonderingly she read their names, pronouncing them the best she could: *Diapason, Euphone Echo, Cor. Anglais, Dolce Corno, Forte, Echo Horn, Celeste, Melodic.*

Pa pushed back his hat and scratched his head. He smiled down at her. "You reckon you could play a little for us?"

For the first time she noticed the stool, covered with turquoise plush. She twirled it and sat down. Opening all the stops, she played a grand chord.

No sound came out.

"Is it broke?" demanded Logan. He and John were almost as excited as she.

She laughed shakily. "I forgot to pump!"

She put her feet on the pedals and pumped, and music poured forth—the most beautiful music she had ever heard.

She found wooden side flaps she could work with her knees to make the notes swell. At first, her fingers did not know where to go because it had been a long time since she had touched organ keys or taken lessons; but after a few trials she could remember "The Snowflake Waltz."

"The organ doesn't sit quite level," Pa remarked. "Son, you run fetch a little piece of wood to stick under this corner."

Logan streaked for the kitchen. In a second he was back—without the wood, his face stamped with astonishment. "Look! Look what I found in the woodbox!"

"What in creation!" gasped Ma.

"Well, I be——" exclaimed Pa.

Lulie managed to tear her gaze from the organ. Logan was clutching something blue with shiny blue buttons. She stared, dumbfounded.

"Where'd them there blue shoes come from?" asked Dave.

"They were in the woodbox!" insisted Logan.

"In the woodbox!" snorted Pa. "I didn't see 'em when I built the fire this morning."

"They were kinda down out of sight."

The blue shoes! The very same ones Trader Shouse had had in his pack last spring and that Lulie had wanted so very much. The beautiful blue shoes that Yarmonite had bought for his squaw.

Lulie reached for them. They were tied together with a

buckskin thong. The soft smooth leather had not a scratch on it.

"Where'd they come from?" she whispered.

The family and Dave surged into the kitchen, peered into the woodbox, flung open the back door.

Tracks! Smudged with the fresh snow, but unmistakable moccasin tracks! And beyond them the trail of a single horse leading down valley.

"Someone was here," growled Pa. "Last night! In the kitchen! A wonder we didn't notice those tracks before. Guess we were just so anxious to get the wagon over——"

"I heard a little noise," remembered Lulie, "and I thought it was a fox."

"It was an Indian!" John's eyes were as big as tomtoms. "He could have scalped us all."

Stupid with amazement, they stood looking at those tracks.

Ma said, "He didn't come to scalp. He came to bring the shoes."

Pa examined the shoes curiously. "What in tunket——" he puzzled. "Any Indian was running a big risk to come up the valley. He'd have been shot if a white man had seen him. And he could have perished in the snow. Just to bring these fool shoes! Why——"

Lulie's voice was tremulous with wonder and comprehension. "Oh, Pa, it wasn't foolish! Don't you see? This is a message from Yarmonite's squaw, and Yarmonite, and

Charlie, and our friends among the Utes to tell us they're still our friends—no matter what!"

"But shoes—I don't——"

"Lulie's right," Ma said. "I remember that day last summer when Yarmonite's squaw came into my kitchen to show us these shoes. They were probably her dearest possession. I expect Yarmonite got some young Indian to bring them. The fellow must have opened the back door and dropped them in the woodbox after he thought we were asleep. Evidently he didn't want to make talk."

"I wish Yarmonite's squaw had kept them," said Lulie. "Oh, I wish she had! Only then we never would have known——"

"They aren't any account," said practical John. "Nobody can wear 'em. Lulie's feet have grown too big."

"No account!" Lulie laid her cheek against the soft blue leather, then had to take her apron and wipe off a tearstain. Marching back into the front room with the family trailing after her, she laid the shoes tenderly on the little shelf above the music rack in the center of the organ.

"I was wishing I could talk to Yarmonite!" Pa's words were gruff. "Maybe this *is* a kind of message."

"Of course it is!" Ma wiped her eyes, unashamed.

By then Aunt Nannie and Sammy had come over from their cabin, and Tommy Bantam had flown up on the carved walnut top of the organ to peer down.

Lulie sat on the stool and began to play, trying to make the music say what she could not say in words. She was thankful for so many things: Pa's safe journey, the organ, and now the blue shoes that were a symbol of a friendship which could outlast trouble. If she made mistakes, nobody paid any attention. She tried slow pieces first, then fast; then Pa reached for the song book, and, opening it, set it on the rack; and they all sang till the blue shoes danced on their shelf, and the sturdy roof beams shook.

How they sang! With shining eyes and flushed cheeks, Lulie played "Amazing Grace" and "Praise Him! Praise Him!" and other favorites. Bear River valley had never heard the like before.

The November wind caught up the music and carried it across the mounds and rushes of old Medicine Springs, that would never again echo to war drum or medicine chant; and on across the snowy sagebrush, where someday would stretch the broad main street of Steamboat Springs.